Girl in a Gar

Girl in a Garden
Lesley Chamberlain

ATLANTIC BOOKS
LONDON

First published in Great Britain in 2003 by Atlantic Books,
an imprint of Grove Atlantic Ltd.

The moral right of Lesley Chamberlain to be identified as the author of this
work has been asserted in accordance with the Copyright, Designs and
Patents Act of 1988.

This novel is entirely a work of fiction. The names, characters and incidents
portrayed in it are the work of the author's imagination. Any resemblance
to actual persons, living or dead, events or localities, is entirely coincidental.

1 3 5 7 9 8 6 4 2

A CIP catalogue record for this book is available from the British Library.

1 84354 102 5

Printed by CPD, Ebbw Vale, Wales.

Atlantic Books
An imprint of Grove Atlantic Ltd
Ormond House
26–27 Boswell Street
London
WC1N 3JZ

I want to give you a mental attitude that in the midst of a totally ordinary existence will keep your life from being botched, so that you will not be a Madame Bovary but an artist, with no regrets or melancholy.

Jean-Paul Sartre, to an early girlfriend

Author's Note

The lines beloved by Henryk Braunschweig on page 69 are by
Bolesław Leśmian. Bettina reads from Revelation ch 22 vv 1–5.

One

Time happens slowly for children. Everything passes in painful detail. Like at school. 'From today Linka Beecham will sit on her own.' Like in the fields behind our house. 'Our mum says you're too rough, Linka. We shouldn't play with you.' Like in our class. 'Linka, you've got boy's hair. We're going to teach you to be a girl.'

I said to Robbie, 'Race you to the jumping tree!' My friend and I forgot everything and everyone and dashed down the grassy slope. Robbie wasn't as fast as I was, but then my mum insisted I always wore wellingtons, because she didn't like the extra work that mud made, so that made us about equal.

The tree had fallen years ago and nothing grew out of it any more. It lay still and stately and dry in the long grass. We thought of it as the remains of a dinosaur. We huffed and puffed our way there and thrust forward with our arms and I threw myself over an invisible finishing line. 'I'm first!'

'That's not fair, Linka. You didn't say where the end was.'

But he let me win. We were friends.

I loved rolling in the old long grass. It was April and the stalks of uncut hay were tough like twine. When the jumping competition began we started at the bottom end of the fallen oak tree and worked upwards, daring each other. I jumped first. By the time we got to the top, which we called the dinosaur's ear, the drop was about seven feet. Wheeee! Yaaaagh! I'm flying. Rosalie and Jonathan Birkett from number thirteen came to join us. It was 1961, I was eleven and we had been in our new house a few months. The Birketts must have been watching out for a good game and Robbie and I always had the best games in the whole of Esper Road. The Birketts were twins and a bit younger than us, stuck for something to do on a Saturday afternoon.

'Come on then, jump!'

Jonathan jumped from the dinosaur's ear and hurt his ankle.

'See what you've done now, Linka Beecham,' said Rosalie, going to him like a mother.

'Jono should learn to jump better.'

Jono sat on the floor and looked wounded.

'You'd be hopeless in a war. They'd drop you behind enemy lines and you'd break your ankle and be no use. But you could learn. You could watch war films on TV. I learn everything from them.'

But the Birketts didn't want my help. 'You're rough, Linka Beecham, everyone says so.'

I made a face at silly, skinny Rosalie, as they went off, and turned to Robbie, who was always there.

'Let's build a den!'

'Yeah, let's be on a desert island like Robinson Crusoe!'

We tramped through the long swathes of neglected grass and bracken until we came to a shallow hollow on the edge of the forest. I could see the line where the fields met the forest from my bedroom window. The point where light switched to dark attracted me. I wanted to dive into it like a pool. When we got nearer, the walking changed. That spot on the edge of the forest was so much like padding over a blanket I wanted to take my shoes off.

Inside the forest the fallen pine needles made the ground soft like felt. And there was a canopy of trees above, just coming into leaf. 'A good place to live!' We dragged over a thick stump to sit on. Woodlice scurried everywhere.

What we couldn't find in nature for our dens we usually found on the building site at the end of the road. We ran up and found a plank all covered in concrete dust, persuaded ourselves that it was old and unwanted, and took it to serve as a table. The evidence for our theft shouted to anyone who passed. The plank dragged back through the grass left a line like an aeroplane wake. We messed the line as best we could. Rolled in it, kicked it. And laughed and clapped.

'Now all we need is a feast!'

Robbie went for pop. I dashed home, felt lucky that I did not encounter my mother, and came back with two Penguins each. We sat on the stump, under the awning of trees, and passed the pop bottle back and forth. 'Cherryade's better.'

'Orange was all we had, Linka. And if my mum catches me...'

We swigged greedily and laughed at each other's orange moustaches. I choked and the orange stuff came out of my nose.

I felt sad then. I sat on the felty ground, with my back against the stump, and wondered what to be. Growing up was a theme at home.

'What do you want to be, Robbie? Do you think your mum and dad knew that one day when they grew up they would go to work in the Washwell factory?'

Robbie's parents made washing machines and fridges, which my mum said was common, she didn't want anything to do with them.

'Well, seeing as the factory didn't exist then...'

'But still. They must have wanted to be something.'

'Work in an office.'

'How awful!'

'Your dad works in an office.'

'I don't think he likes it. I would like to work on a farm. Only they're building houses on all the fields now because there aren't enough nice places for people to live. So perhaps I'll be a builder.'

'But you're a girl!'

'So?'

Dad had told me that thousands of houses like ours were being built so people could lead more beautiful lives away from London. The capital was old and dark and poor. 'After the war', the time we lived in, people thought of beauty often. They thought of people leading beautiful lives because there had been so much ugliness. It would be a fine thing to be a builder.

'You can't be a builder.' Robbie looked smug. 'But I can be something good. I'm going to design aeroplanes and fly round the world.'

'*You* could design a magic plane to fly you back in time. Then I could be a time traveller. I'd like that even more than being a builder.'

'Why can't *I* be the time traveller?'

'Because I know about the past and you don't.' I believed in my divining powers. 'Think of it, Robbie. We're living with the ghost of Esper House. All this once belonged to one rich family.' I stood up on the stump and scanned the crest of the hill. In my hands I held an imaginary telescope, but I did not see with my eyes.

'I wonder what it was like when everything belonged to the people of Esper House. They had this huge garden with a greenhouse and other buildings. And ponies in the fields beyond and maybe a lake with boats.'

'No lake, Linka. You can't have a lake on top of a hill.'

Uncovering the past would be a job. I would like that job. Robbie wasn't going to take it away from me with his mean-mindedness. I jumped down and was going to swipe him one for denying me a lake when suddenly there was a crackle in the undergrowth. We stopped. We thought it was a fox. Then I saw a red jumper. It was Sen, the farmhand. Esper Road had been built on two of his boss's fields. Sen was sometimes around, sometimes not, helping 'the boss'.

'Heeee, Linka! What's that you've got there? Pop?'

Robbie looked stony-faced at the dark, scruffy farm boy, who had mean, sharp features and thin lips.

I noticed the rifle. 'Have you been shooting rabbits, Sen?'

'I have that, Linka. Pesky things. Now, what are you two kids doin', hidin' here in the woods? Not playing mums and dads, I 'ope.' He winked.

'Go away,' said Robbie.

'Why're you so unfriendly to poor Sen? 'e's only come to see 'is Linka.'

Sen reached over and tipped our bottle to his lips.

'Because I am.' Robbie poured away the rest.

'Heehee, you made a puddle, Robbie. I could 'ave done that for yer.'

'Go away.'

'Bye, Sen,' I called.

'Why are you nice to him? He's dirty.'

But I liked the way Sen appeared and vanished like a ghost, going nowhere and belonging nowhere, disappearing into the woods. He had a home no one knew about.

I sat down on the log. 'I'd like to live in the forest. I want to build a hut and live here for ever.'

'What about Sen? You couldn't keep him away.'

'He'd lend me his rifle to protect myself, I know he would.'

'What about school?'

'I'd still go. And I'd get the postman to call. And the popman. It would be a proper place.'

'Don't you like your house?'

'I do, I do. But I wish it had wheels. I wish Esper Road was all on wheels, like in *Wagon Train*. Imagine, Robbie, we're pioneers from the East. We're travelling across America to find the Promised Land. We find a hillside to shelter us and stop for the night. When we wake up and climb to the top before breakfast we see we've happened on a beautiful place. The cry goes up, let's settle here! And the people line up their wagons like our houses are lined up in Esper Road, and the settlers are happy that they no longer have to travel, and they dig gardens and grow corn.'

'Maybe we could build a wagon.'

'No, silly, it's just a thought.'

But what a thought! The Promised Land! I felt that about Esper Road. I would stand for hours staring out of our garden at number seventeen, through the ridge of ash trees which bordered it, contemplating the green valley and the forest which rose beyond. I knew what it was to want to build a beautiful life. And for me, much of that had to do with living outdoors.

'*My* mum wouldn't allow me to live outdoors.'

'She could come to visit. I would let my mum and dad come to visit.'

'Your mum lets you do anything.'

I thought about that. It didn't make sense. So I said, 'Let's go back to the dinosaur. Dare you to jump off the ear again. Barefoot.' And off we went.

'Easy peasy.' Robbie jumped first to show his mettle and next minute I was back in flight too. I was crumpling up on the ground, breaking my fall, not like some feeble Jono Birkett but like a real expert parachutist. I wasn't fighting now, just dropping down through the air for the adventure of it, for the sensation in falling, and the shock when I landed. Barefoot was great and barelegged too. I rolled up my cotton trousers above the knee. Now I could *feel* any stones that might be lurking under the grass. We jumped and jumped, and threw ourselves over on the ground as we landed. I yearned to collide with something hard and sharp. I didn't know why until suddenly my knee was bleeding. Then I knew. I drank in that bright red, a shining lake of living me, spreading into rivulets along the folds of my skin, and looked up in triumph.

'Ooh, Linka, it looks nasty. Don't you want to cry?'

I shook my head.

We sat on the low end of the giant oak trunk. It was already warm in the April sunshine. I straddled our dinosaur, while I watched the blood congeal and darken on my knee. The bark of the oak had deep rills which dug into my thighs. Ants ran along its dark, high-walled paths. I could imagine being a tiny ant, trying to find the way out of the maze.

'Our dinosaur is the Grand Canyon for that ant.'

'Bet you don't know where the Grand Canyon is.' Robbie's pale face was bony and his bright little eyes glittered. We were friends.

I did. I knew it from TV, from *Wagon Train*. I nodded my head.

'Where is the Grand Canyon then?'

'Anywhere. Look. This one. She's looking for the way home. Up this street, up that one. It's always wrong.'

'He'll never get out.'

I squealed. 'You heard what I said. It's a she, and *she* will get out. Girls are better than boys!' *You've got boy's hair. We're going to teach you to be a girl. From today Linka Beecham will sit on her own.*

I felt sad again. Robbie saw it and pressed home his chance.

'Aren't you ever afraid, Linka?'

'No!' I grabbed his shoulders and made a frightening face, sticking my rigid tongue up his nose. 'No, I'm not afraid. There's nothing to be afraid of in the world if you are a strong person.' I twisted his arm as I let him go, and he said, with the mist-filled eyes he often had, that I didn't have to do that. *Our mum says you're too rough, Linka. We shouldn't play with you.*

Susan Birkett overheated her house and overfilled it with things, including three young children. The youngest, Timmy, was what they called backward and this made the older twins, Jonathan and Rosalie, sober and responsible at too young an age.

Jono wanted to be a good boy, and he was, but he didn't have the intelligence to match. His eyes were bright and deep, but his expression was dull. He had to be a good boy and that meant being a careful boy. He should not lose things because of the oxygen Timmy had lost at birth. He should not be untidy, because fate had been most untidy in designing Timmy.

Rosalie, for her part, had put away her dolls as soon as she learned the truth about Timmy. On top of that she divined something about her father, which made her her mother's devoted helper.

Red-faced Bob Birkett brimmed with charity towards the world but was mostly out of the house. He worked as a reporter and editor on the local paper. Local politics kept him a willing hostage. Number thirteen Esper Road was overheated and untidy and Susan was often tired and didn't make much of herself. But Bob saw himself as a devoted husband and that made him behave like one, whether he was home or not, so all at the Birketts was well. The stability attracted. Emma Beecham often popped round to see Susan.

Emma didn't mind the heat and closed her eyes to the mess. So long as the Birkett children were at school or in bed, she didn't care. She only didn't like children. She had reached a stage in her marriage, or her life, when she could bear silence no longer. She could bear this marriage no longer. She couldn't get up in the morning, she felt restless all day, she could not bear the sight of her daughter Lynne-Caroline's clutter: the old bones and the loose stamps. She needed a confessor. She sometimes forgot that the child could hear.

'The child is rough. She behaves like a boy. Charles hates it and complains to me, but what am I supposed to do? Neither of us can understand why we have produced such an uncouth child.

'I took her shopping the other day. She needs things. She's growing up. But I had to drag her there and then she made a scene in the ladieswear department, pretending to be sick. I like pretty clothes but she refuses to take an interest. I had her chest measured in the Foundation Department. 32 A! I bought her her first bra, a lovely thing in white cotton, and she refuses to wear it.'

'It'll pass, Emma, it's just a stage. My kids say she's brainy at school. You must be thankful for that.'

'Thankful? I don't know. It makes her queer. She's always asking about the past. I went to hoover her room the other day. There were stamps all over the floor. I found a lot of bones under the bed. She saved a trout bone from our dinner down at the Palace Hotel. And then I unwrapped her pyjamas and found the skull of some creature, together with a note: FRAGILE! DO NOT BREAK.'

Susan laughed. 'Kids will be kids.'

'I said to Charles she should go away to school. But he says we can't afford it, that we already live beyond our means.'

'You and Charles are the best off in our street apart from the Emsworths.'

'They're very young. Ten years younger than us, I'd say. They won't stay here long. He's a solicitor just qualified. I wish Charles was a professional like Stephen Emsworth. I wish we were rich.'

'You're wishing for more than you need, Emma. You have a lovely husband and a beautiful house, fine clothes and a clever daughter.'

'I want to be RICH, RICH I SAY!' Emma doubled her

message with some force. 'And a daughter like Linka is not a blessing if she can't be sent away to school. To be rich would be the solution to everything.'

Oh! Oh. Susan Birkett was shocked and retreated into a few moments' silence. She picked up some darning she had been stabbing at before Emma rang the chimes. 'Have you thought about a part-time job? That would give you interest and a bit of extra money.'

'I don't like work. When I was a child we had servants.'

'Emma dear, you're full of regrets for your childhood.'

'It was the best time of my life, before the war.'

'But surely you can hardly remember it?'

'It was the best time.' Emma dissolved in reverie. 'Even with Dorothy there. Dorothy, my older sister, was a bit like your Timmy. No, much worse, she couldn't even sit up straight or talk properly. But I liked her being there. I used to make up things for her to say.' In her mind Emma was back in that tall, gloomy, red-brick house on three floors in the London suburb where the Luck-Carters had lived.

'But when my father lost his money, first we got rid of Cook and Nurse, then Mother had Dorothy put away. Mother said life was cruel and one shouldn't try to disguise it. We couldn't look after a moron any more, not with our diminished means. We could barely keep body and soul together in ourselves. Dorothy being abandoned just like that made me afraid. It was like putting her in a cupboard and closing the door.'

Susan felt sorry for Emma. She knew what family meant. It meant just those things like not sending a deformed child away, whatever blows arrived from the outside world. She told her new neighbour from number seventeen, the one with the rough child, 'I'm glad you feel you can come round.'

Emma began to cry.

Robbie said, 'Your parents are rich. Look at the clothes your mum wears! Your dad holds an umbrella over her head all the way up the garden path when it's raining. I saw him the other day when you were going out shopping. My mum said—'

'How do you know we're *rich*?'

'Your mum likes to show she's different from everyone else.'

'You don't know. You're just gossiping.'

'Shut up!'

'You shut up!' My satchel hung over one shoulder, but I shoved Robbie with the other and he fell off the curb. 'You're all skin and bones,' I said, imitating what adults said about him. It was a victory for one day. But the problem didn't go away.

Another friend from school, Alan Robertson, said we were posh. I felt terrible.

'Are we posh, Dad? Are we rich?'

'Oh no', Dad replied. 'Wherever did you get that idea from, Linka? Only very few people in this country are rich and in fact far too many are poor. Britain isn't a fair place. Though now the war's over it's going to get much better because people have realized just how unfair it used to be. A few people had big houses and gardens, but most had nothing at all.'

'Like Esper House,' I said. 'Now Esper House is for all of us.'

'Exactly.' But he sounded uncertain.

'But posh, Dad, aren't we posh? What about Mum's clothes? And her holidays to special places. That's what most people only dream about, Robbie's mum said.' And I told him about what Alan said.

'Look, Linka, everyone is special in their own way. Otherwise, we Beechams are just ordinary people and that's as things should be.'

'Of course, Dad.' But I started to watch our life at number seventeen Esper Road. And I tried to go home to other people's homes from school to find out how their lives differed from ours.

'Good afternoon, Mrs Robertson.'

'Well, you must be Linka. Come and sit here, dear.'

Alan and I had walked from school to his tiny house, one of four in a row, made from some strange material that pinged when you tapped it with your fingernail. Without a word Alan himself showed me how to ping it. It was a gesture he had somehow acquired to salute the soul of the place called Westcross Row.

Mrs Robertson, a tall woman who was brisk in her movements, pulled out a chair for me at the dark brown wooden table.

'Linka's an unusual name, isn't it? But it's nice. It sounds very modern.'

She looked much older than my mother and she smelt of cigarette smoke. She wore a pinafore tied round her neck and waist. My mum wouldn't have approved of a woman presenting herself as a domestic servant, no matter how voluntarily, and because of that, so many sensations of strangeness overwhelmed me I couldn't speak, not even to explain my name.

'So how do you like it at Arlingham with Miss Rogers? She's a dragon and no mistake. Alan's seen her fire a few times, haven't you, Al?'

I remained silent out of deep confusion. I was a good girl,

who liked our headmistress, even if she did put me on my own because I had top marks. *From today Linka Beecham will sit on her own.* It was a terrible moment when Miss Rogers, with her pale face and pale hair and little gold glasses, strode into our classroom in her squeaky flat shoes, brushing our teacher aside. Everyone looked at me when she made the announcement and Bettina whispered something to make Danny laugh.

'No need to be shy with us, Linka,' began Mrs Robertson. 'We're nothing special. Now, you've just moved here, or do I tell a lie?'

A lie? What a word! I hated that word. I associated it with my mother's dreams.

'We moved in after Christmas and my birthday. That's the truth,' I said, then I asked what happened to Mrs Robertson during the war.

She said that was an unexpected question and got up stiffly to make us some tea.

I looked around. The little room where we were sitting was quite dark. There was a heavy sideboard and some chairs with dark wooden arms and a matching settee with flowery covers and lots of glass ornaments and photographs on the sideboard, and little pictures on the wall. Everything was quite different from our house, which had bright colours and big windows. I thought of our red rug with its pattern of yellow, blue and black sticks in one corner, and our turquoise chair, and our French windows leading on to the patio and the garden beyond. We had more light and more space. We lived in luxury. This was something less. Mrs Robertson brought us milky tea and jam sandwiches. I prayed they wouldn't make me sick.

Mrs Robertson said she'd been a child like me when the war

broke out. She had helped on her uncle's farm. Were we doing a project on the war at school? What made me so curious about the war? she asked. I shook my head.

The tea tasted of cheap, sterilized milk, whereas we always had fresh. Dad said people bought sterilized milk if they didn't have fridges, because it kept longer. I found myself hoping that the Robertsons could buy a fridge from Washwell when they got richer. Alan kicked me under the table and I kicked him back. We weren't having enough fun. I wondered whether it would be all right to leave half my tea.

'So what did you two do today at school?'

'Nothing, Mum, it was boring.'

'Now, Alan Robertson, that's not an answer.'

I took a deep breath. 'Miss did an experiment. She showed us oil and water bursting into flames. We talked about fire. I said...' And I was off on a wave of enthusiasm for the elements. Fire, water, earth and air, I loved them all. And I loved school. But neither of the Robertsons was interested in my story of the science experiment. A blue-breasted budgerigar in a cage began chirruping. 'Is he singing because he's happy? How do you know if a bird is happy?'

Mrs Robertson gave me a long look and shooed us outside to play. I said I needed to spend a penny but she told me that was outside too. Alan led me round into the back garden and pointed to a wooden door. I had to stand on the seat to reach the chain.

A huge buckety-watery racket followed in my wake. Alan put a finger to his lips. I protested it wasn't my fault and laughed out loud. He smiled and made us tiptoe to the end of the garden. I think he was pretending his animals were babies.

'So where is it then?' I peered into the box where the stoat was supposed to be. 'Look, Al, look, it's not there. It's escaped! I know, your stoat's a prisoner of war and it's escaped.'

I had seen some film, some war film, on TV. We stood, bent over the cardboard box, which had a hole in the side. Cardboard crumbs had fallen in a neat pile on the concrete slab. The stoat, which I suspected had been caught only very recently for my benefit, hadn't stayed long with the Robertsons.

'I'll get another one,' said Alan.

'What did it look like?'

'Small, furry.'

'He or she?'

'She.'

'And the slowworm?' He pointed to a thin, shiny snake about eight inches long which lay curled on some dry grass in an old paintpot with air holes punched in the side. I crouched over it, looking for a sign of life. Alan bent over too.

'Will you be my friend, Linka?'

'I don't know.' I loved Alan. I also loved Robbie. But to say it?

Mrs Robertson appeared. 'Alan, there's a dear, run down and get me some ciggies. Get yourselves some sweets while you're there.'

'Do you like my mum?'

'Yes.'

I forgave her for not listening to my news from school. My own mum didn't either. We walked back along the grass path and down the asphalt road to buy Mrs Robertson ten Players No 10.

'What's your mum's name?'

'Ellie.' Then Alan added, 'We're not posh like you.'

I said recklessly, 'That's true. My dad says it's scandalous there are any prefabs left in Brightsea a whole sixteen years after the end of the war.'

'What's it to do with your dad?'

'He does politics. He says everyone's entitled to a decent place to live.'

'We like it here.'

'You'll still have to move. My dad said it's about progress.'

'We'll see about that'. Alan snorted, pushed hard against the glass door of the newsagent's and went in first.

The opening door rang a bell. From inside the shop, if you turned round, you could see the bronze dome hanging on a high bracket with the tongue inside still swaying back and forth. A tall man with swept-back dark hair and a thin face appeared from out the back. He had large hands with a dirty sticking plaster on one finger and a red pencil behind his ear. Alan handed him a note written on lined paper from his mum and a silver florin. The shopkeeper shook his head as he picked the white-blue-green box off the shelf behind the counter. The cigarettes were 1/10d and he wasn't allowed to sell them to children. But he'd lose half his trade if he didn't help out the mums stuck at home.

Raising his voice from a mutter he asked, 'Anything else?'

'Something each for a penny.' There was a special section of the sweet counter divided into glass troughs, each one full of farthing and halfpenny and penny treats. You couldn't buy the farthing sweets singly any more because the government had abolished farthings in the same month as my birthday, but you could make up a bagful. Alan had four blackjacks and I had a sherbet puffball.

'I hope you lads are honest,' the man called, as the bell tinkled again. He meant he hoped we weren't going to smoke the ciggies ourselves. I was considering my treat, bringing it towards my mouth and had even got to the moment, which I knew very well, of touching my tongue against what seemed to be a yellow cardboard flying saucer, got to the first moment when the sherbet bit into my tongue and fizzed, when my heart leapt out of my chest. *Heh! I'm not a lad. I'm not a boy.* I opened the door of the shop and shut it again in quick succession, three times. Tinkle tinkle tinkle.

'You'd think the fire brigade was coming,' said Alan. We giggled.

'Oi, stop that!' The shopkeeper made a couple of steps towards us but we'd gone.

'Do I look like a boy?'

Alan laughed. 'You're a girl but you like doing boys' things.'

'So? They're more interesting.' We took the No 10s back to Mrs Robertson. Then I picked up my blazer and satchel, said thank you for having me and left.

Neither Mum nor I would forget that recent trip to Jennings in a hurry. As a memento the white bra was stuffed to the back of my drawer along with some frilly knickers she gave me for my birthday. I'd had a plan to resist going shopping with her. I'd seen the Ban the Bomb protesters on TV, sitting in the road. When they didn't want the policemen to move them on they let their whole bodies go limp and refused to move. I tried it. But I wasn't big enough. She just dragged me to the bus stop and into Jennings.

The lift, or, as I knew from TV that Americans called it, the elevator, was all made of polished wood and it had a bronze trellis that snapped shut across the front like a hundred pairs of handcuffs. It went a bit fast as it landed, and made your tummy jump. But after that bit of fun, well! Down with Jennings Department Store! Bulldoze it! Build a field! I could imagine no more lifeless place than this vast walk-in wardrobe where we went two or three times a year, and which was always too hot. My clothes itched and I sweated in winter, while in summer I felt parched and *truly* headachy and longed to get out into the fresh air. The ladieswear department smelt vaguely of starch and thread and the mingled perfumes of circulating customers and staff. The only relief was to screw up my eyes, when I could see a big square park with straight rows of flowering bushes, and my different kind of mother fluttering like a butterfly from one bush to the next.

'Oh, now, isn't that beautiful? Don't you think that's a beautiful outfit for a young girl?'

While I writhed beside her, attempting various feats of balance and contortion, for I truly did not want a dress or a skirt, Mum's hand, tipped with five bloody daggers of nail polish, flitted from hanger to hanger. Now and again she would push one back against the pile and smooth the front of a jacket or a dress, or in this case, a combination of the two.

The saleswoman hovered beside us, suggesting my mother might like to carry her fantasy one step further and try the outfit on me. I wanted to shout, Get off us! Leave us alone! But I could only scowl.

'It's very well made too!'

'I think it would just suit her.'

My big hazel eyes went up into my head and I clutched my stomach. My mouth hung open. 'Have you got a bin?' I cried.

'I'm going to be sick.' The assistant rushed me across the room and beside the staff desk bent me double over a metal wastepaper bin. It smelt of apple core. I looked down and saw a tangle of human hair sticking to the discarded yellow-brown fruit. My stomach had no hesitation in pumping out its contents.

My mother said, 'Oh leave her, she's always doing that. It's just to annoy me and her father that she pretends she's a boy. My husband calls her Peter Pan. There, you see, she's not even content to be Wendy.' Mum wandered over to a rail of adult dresses. 'Now, that's lovely for me. I could wear it in the evenings in Spain.'

I breathed silently: Mum, Mum! Stop lying!

The saleswoman gasped. 'Are you going to Spain for your holidays?' To go abroad was expensive. With that kind of money my mother might really buy something. But the saleswoman didn't want to give the impression of being lower down the social scale so she faked knowing all about it. 'They say Ibi-ts-ia is quite unspoilt. Will you be going there or to the Costa Brava?'

I finally found my voice. 'When are we going to Spain?'

Mum sprang back at me. 'Not you. I'm going. I'm going alone. And you can't stop me.'

I turned to the assistant. 'Normally we go to Cornwall in a caravan, you know. And it usually rains.'

My mother put her arm round me so that her hand covered my mouth. She cast a second, unhappy glance at the beautiful dress and said she would think about it. Then off we went to the Foundation Department, where they strapped me into a brassiere.

'Hello, I'm home. Where's Dad?'

I was unlacing my school shoes with one hand, holding the door to the kitchen open with the other. The spring in the handle twanged so funnily I pressed it down a few times to make the sound again. Nnungh, nnungh, nnungh, as if the door was chewing. Otherwise, the small space in which we kept boots and coats, and which opened in the other direction into the downstairs toilet, made me impatient to pass through. It was cramped and the doormat prickled my feet through my socks.

'Here you are at last.' My mother stood in the kitchen, not helping me but looking me over with disapproval. I heard her sigh. 'Goodness!'

'Hi, Mum, where's Dad?' I repeated.

'Good Heavens, I heard you the first time, Lynne-Caroline. He's out at one of his meetings.' She always called me by my proper name, though to everyone else I was Linka.

'Is it a meeting about prefabs? Are they going to force the people in the prefabs to move so we can all forget about the war? Dad says we should forget all about the war. I mean, it was a pity that the Germans bombed Brightsea and even more of a pity that some of the bombs missed the docks and hit people's houses and left great craters in the street, but these things happen. That's why he's learning German, to be friends again.'

'What are you talking about?'

I repeated my question about prefabs, to which my mum shook her head. The china plate spun on the table where she tossed it. When it stopped she laid on it a slab of buttered toast and topped it with some reheated baked beans.

'Wash your hands first! Outside!' She bossed me so I was back among the boots. She immersed the scraped saucepan in some water in the sink and sat down opposite me.

'What happened to you in the war, Mum?'

'Lynne-Caroline, not that story again, please.' She sighed and put her hands to her cheeks. 'Is your tea nice? Didn't they give you anything round at your friend's?'

'Jam sandwiches.'

'You'd better go up for a bath afterwards. You look filthy.'

'Mum, in the war, did you ever hear an air raid siren?'

Of course she had. But only twice, because after that she got sent to the country. Granny knew better what happened in London. Granny was in London throughout the war. Nothing stopped Granny. She loved adventures. The Powells were always a tough breed. Except for the exceptions. Like Dorothy. I had digested my mother's words many times and had long decided that Granny was my heroine and I would be of the tough breed. But it's not fair, Granny's dead. I can't ask her.

'But Mum! Tell me about when you were sent to the country to be safe.'

'I hated every moment.'

'But why, Mum, why? The country's nice. Wasn't it like Esper Road?'

'No.'

'Was it posh?'

'No.' She began to sing over the washing-up so I couldn't ask her any more questions.

'Mum, Mum, Mrs Robertson's not half as pretty...'

But she wasn't listening. With her face fixed on the dark kitchen window out on to the street, and her hands working clumsily in rubber gloves, she reminded me of Mrs Robertson's budgie, stuck behind net curtains, unable to see the world outside, so having to make it up, only Mum was singing 'Some Enchanted

Evening' which was 'a song from a show'. My dear mummy.

'She's a lonely child. Charles says it's our fault. But I don't want another child. Besides, I was lonely too, on that farm, with that cruel woman Pickles and her little Ralph and Margot. I remember it as yesterday. I was evacuated on the twenty-sixth of September 1940. They pinned a label on me with my name, Emma Luck-Carter, and my date of birth: 14 November, 1927. My Lincolnshire parents, as I was supposed to call them. I remember the taste of that soup made of leftovers.'

My mum was often out. At Susan's. At the pictures.

When Mum was out Dad and I drove in our Anglia to get fish and chips. Inside Andy's the frying fish sizzled in the huge stainless steel bath and the whole place was warm. I hugged the warm counter. We often had to wait because Andy's were the best fish and chips for miles around. Sometimes there was a queue of half a dozen people. But Dad never got angry or impatient. Under the bright strip light he looked handsome and kind, a bit like Clint Eastwood on TV. Now and again we saw someone he knew. A man called Dad 'Beech'. Two women called him 'Charlie'.

'Eat now or take away?'

'Salt and vinegar to take away,' replied Dad, passing me the warm parcel which I held in my lap all the way home. When we got in, he heated up a couple of plates for us in the oven, along with the unwrapped package. Then we spread the feast on our laps in the sitting room and watched television. He sat in the turquoise chair we called the modern one (chosen by my mum) and I sat on the floor beside him, leaning against his knees.

'Dad, if you had one wish in the world, what would it be?'

'I'd wish you to grow up successful and happy, Linka.'

Oh no. *From today Linka Beecham will sit on her own.*

'Mum wants me to grow up *now*. She wants to be free. She told the woman in Jennings she was going to Spain. She was going without us and wanted something very special and glamorous, for the evenings in Spain.'

Dad sighed deeply. I felt the air flow out of him and fill his body again in a great heave and I was glad I wasn't looking at him. 'Your mother likes to dream,' he said finally. 'That's part of what makes her unusual.'

'Charles doesn't understand the needs of a modern woman. I'm a modern woman. I don't want to spend my time skivvying. I want an interesting life. Some adventure. Just something different. I go to the pictures on my own just to see a different world, to get out of Esper Road.'

'You need a job, Emma, really.'

'But I have a child to look after. I could only get a job if she went away!'

'You're not telling the truth.'

'It's true she hardly needs me. She plays outside for hours. I hardly see her except when she's hungry. And yet I don't want a job. When I was young we had servants.'

I *was* free. I stood among among the slim perpendiculars of the ash trees at the end of our garden and felt the smooth coolness and the firmness of their friendly trunks. I was eleven and free. The trees made me free. They said, 'Come on now, Linka, don't be scared. Take our hands. That's it. And lift! There!' The young ash branches trembled like acrobats whenever I accepted their outstretched offer but they never let me down. I stood on a thicket of twigs with my arms outstretched and leaned so far forwards that I flew over the field, down towards the forest, and though I still had my feet in Esper Road, my stomach soared into the air. I was flying on Robbie's Time Machine!

Or I went up to my room where I kept the skull of a cat under my bed, wrapped in my pyjamas. I had found it in the fields and it was too good to put on the class nature table. I sat on the floor with pussy's skull in my lap and read a library book about the war and found stamps from my collection for the countries that were in the war. I never stuck them in an album and they blew away. But I liked stamps. I liked the words on the stamps which I couldn't understand.

'So many people had nowhere to live, Linka. All the big towns and cities in the Midlands and the south were bombed.'

'Did people get killed in Brightsea?'

Dad nodded and told me about air raid sirens and underground shelters. Then I saw a programme about the Blitz on TV and I heard air raid sirens in my dreams. London was bombed every night from October to December 1940. Parts of Brightsea, especially around the docks, still stood empty, with weeds growing out of broken walls and puddles and mounds of blackish earth where tall warehouses had been.

'Heh, pussy, did you live in the war? What was it like? Did you get killed by a bomb? Did a house fall on you? Or did they just leave you behind when they moved from Esper House? It was too much trouble to evacuate cats. Go to sleep again now pussy.'

On my knees I turned to the old wireless I was dismantling with the help of Dad's screwdriver. I thought I could make it work again if I made the right connections. Downstairs on our proper radio I had heard the foreign talk of all those faraway places marked on the dial. Hilversum and Oslo, Berlin and Warsaw. They were all in the war. They might be able to tell me something about what it was like.

'If you trip over that wireless in the dark you'll hurt yourself.'

'I've got a torch, Dad, it'll be OK.'

I lay in the dark. I could hear my wristwatch with the Roman numerals ticking. Dad's birthday present. It sounded as if it was playing a tune. But I didn't know any words to it, so over the top I sang very quietly the first verse of my favourite hymn: 'Praise My Soul the King of Heaven'. Then I played with a few words and phrases like progress and disarmament and economic miracle and independent nuclear deterrent, which I'd heard – from Dad, on the news, somewhere – but couldn't remember the meaning of. My head was a jumble of sounds and memories, all of them wriggling and alive like the diseases we had looked at under a microscope at school. It was a good school. 'Progressive,' they said.

Just before I went up to bed, we had been sitting round the TV. Mum was wearing her pink and white nightie. Dad turned up the sound and we watched the news. We always did watch the news. We sat close to each other because the TV screen was so small. But we weren't close. We didn't share our thoughts. We each had our separate secrets. Dad was thinking about 'his politics'. They were like a cupboard where Mum had shut him in. Mum was admiring the suit, the figure, the face, in fact everything there was to admire about Jacqueline Kennedy, the wife of the American President, who was like a film star, a beautiful woman with long, dark, flicked-up hair. She smiled and waved to the crowd on our black-and-white screen about the size of a biscuit box.

We're sitting here like misers, I thought. Misers was a new word and I liked it because I could make it mean something. My head chanted the nursery rhyme which said that the king was in his counting-house counting out his money and the queen was in her parlour eating bread and honey. But we were counting not money on a table but secrets in our heads.

Then they were shouting in the bedroom next door. I hated that. I crept out to the spare bedroom, the only one which faced on to Esper Road, and signalled to Robbie: SOS. SOS. Three short, three long, three short. You heard it a lot in war films, broadcast by the radio officer when the ship was in trouble. The camera always showed his fingers pressing hard on the signal button.

'Linka, what are you doing?' There stood my gentle dad in his crimson pyjamas, in the doorway of the spare room, where I had opened the window and was leaning out. 'Sleep now. Go back to bed.'

Esper Road wasn't finished. There were twenty-six houses now but eventually there would be double that, and the builders worked every weekday and gradually spread out into the fields. They dug a pit right down near our den. I heard stoats squeaking there. I told Alan and he came over after school. The clocks had changed. The evenings were longer. We picked our way over uneven clods of dried earth and stones, a kind of path from the building site to the pit.

'Your mum looks like a film star.'

'When did you see her?'

'At school. When she came up about O'Brien's shed.'

We had been in trouble over 'O'Brien's shed' and Miss Rogers summoned all the parents. My mother must have wanted to show off her clothes. She wouldn't have come near our school otherwise. She told me she hated school. She stood in the long corridor outside Miss Rogers's office, in her yellow linen dress and jacket, making all the other mothers look dowdy. She seemed to say to people, Look at you all, your lives are so dull! Miss Rogers held a meeting in a corner of the assembly hall, where she outlined our crimes. In her flat shoes and tweed skirt and with the bunch of keys at her waist unfortunately she looked like a jailer.

'Gestapo,' Mum whispered. 'Could have run a concentration camp by the looks of it.'

'Steady on!' Mrs O'Brien whispered back. 'I'm sorry she's making so much fuss.'

Mum and Mrs Robertson didn't speak and only exchanged looks in secret.

'Mum says she's ahead of her time. People will see. The time will come when more people are like her, and not thought of as odd at all.'

I tried to ape mum's little cat face and her way of talking about herself as if she were dancing or as if she were a TV presenter showing off the prizes that could be won. There was a show, *Double Your Money*. She must have got it from that. She thought of herself as a prize for someone, somehow.

'She's progressive.' I wasn't sure what that word meant but we heard it a lot. 'Progressive is like modern.'

'Is your dad progressive too?'

Somehow that made me laugh. 'I expect not. What about yours?'

'We're not posh like you.'

'What's that got to do with it?'

'I don't know. But I'm sure.'

I didn't deny the poshness, for posh in my mind had a slight connection with being fashionable and modern, which the Robertsons weren't. Posh also reflected the airs and graces my mum put on to impress other people. But in the end I knew our family was just different from Alan's, so I stopped talking. We sat down in the grass.

'My dad says you're going to be *rehoused* soon.'

'We don't want to go. How would you like to be forced to move?'

'But we live in a proper house.'

'You're a snob.'

'But you could live in a beautiful new place.' Dad, I had discovered, was on the Council.

'I think your dad should mind his own business.'

That was difficult. I loved Dad and I loved Alan, but only an extra dimension in my thoughts would fit them both in. 'You know Al, I don't believe in the future and progress. I think everything is with us all the time ... in the woods and in the sky, and before and after and during the war, and in Poland and here, now—'

'Where's Poland?'

'Where the man from number fourteen comes from. Haven't you heard about Poland? It's where Hitler invaded, what started the war.' I added, laughing, 'You should know about the war. Then you'd know why you're living in a prefab.' I heard Miss Roger's voice: 'You'll go to university, Linka. I'm proud of you. Just tell me why a girl like you went with the boys to O'Brien's shed?'

'Show-off,' said Alan.

We sat again in silence.

I suddenly hurled myself on to him. 'They're shelling us. Geddown!' I felt his heart beating under me, as the whine and ping of ballistic assault filled my ears. Then silence in the air. I raised my head cautiously, as trained warriors do. No blood. All limbs still intact. I pulled a little round mirror with a plastic back from my pocket. Breath was still issuing from both our lips. I rolled off and we listened in perfect stillness. 'All clear. They've gone.' In my palm I revealed a spent cartridge, which had been digging into my back as we lay in the grass. 'Sen shooting rabbits.'

'Doubtless.'

'My dad says there was nearly another war when I was six. No one wants another war. That's why all those people march in the streets and shout at policemen.'

'You go on and on about the war, Linka.' He stood up.

'So? If there were another war you'd have to fight, Al. You'd probably get killed.'

'Yeah, probably I would.' He went to fetch his schoolbag from where we had begun further up the hill, before the Germans shelled us. Halfway up he turned back. 'But you're the one who likes fighting, Linka. I think they'd get a special army full of girls like you, and make them go first.'

I turned on my stomach to watch him. Sucking the sweet end of a blade of grass, to be like Al, for that was what he did, I accepted what he said.

He produced two jam jars with holes punched in the lids. 'Let's catch the stoats!'

We trundled over to the spot and lay down on the crusty red soil with our heads hanging over the pit. Almost immediately

Robbie hooted to signal he was on his way. I trumpeted back. Da-dut-der-der!

'Shut up, Robbie! You're so stupid and fussy!'

But I blocked Al's complaints. 'There's plenty of time, Al. Robbie, did you bring the pop?'

He did. He was always reliable.

The three of us now hung over the dark narrow pit. It was as if a giant apple corer had removed a piece of the field. It must have been twenty feet deep and smelt rotten. We sat up again and passed round the bottle. I said I would go for the rope.

The sun was still visible, streaked with blood like one of those 'fertilized' eggs you sometimes got on your breakfast plate. It hung like the yellow gong of the chief god of the world. I hauled myself up through the ash trees into our garden, chundered into the garage in my wellingtons, slung the heavy tow rope round me and ran back over the bumpy ground downhill.

The boys were sitting cross-legged, in silence.

'I've got the rope.'

'Great.'

'They're there now. Can you hear them squeaking?'

'Yeah.' My heart skipped a beat.

'It's like noises your mum and dad make at night.'

'Yeah, that's right.'

'You're lying, Linka,' said Robbie.

'I'm not. Just because yours don't make those noises. Just because yours are so old.'

'And a jolly good thing. What a stupid noise for anyone to make. People aren't animals.'

I was about to hurl myself on Robbie when I noticed Al tying the rope in a reef knot under his arms to form a cradle.

'Stop, Al, it's me who's going.'

'But you're a girl.'

'I'm just as strong as you. Anyway I got the rope. Gimme that jar.'

The boys held the rope, Robbie in second place. Al, with bent knees, leaned back and slowly let out the slack from the coil behind him. '*Walk* down the side! Go down as if you were walking!'

'I can't walk. The soil's falling in my eyes. I'll just dangle. Lemme down some more.'

'The rope hurts,' cried Robbie. 'It's burning my hands. I'm going to have to let go.'

'You dare,' warned Al. I felt sorry for Robbie.

'Linka, you OK?' he shrieked.

'Yeah.' I landed on the wet floor of the soil well and saw nothing but giant walls of wet earth all around me.

Al called down, 'What's it like?'

'Cold. Really deep. Now, shhh.'

Back up on the surface, far above my head, the birdsong of the evening sounded like the whole of assembly singing 'Praise My Soul the King of Heaven'. Perhaps God saw the world like this. Or perhaps this is what it was like to be dead. I crouched, hands cupped. And tipped the slithering creature into the jar.

'OK! Got one! Pull me up.'

The boys readied the rope.

'I don't know if I can do it. It's harder on the way up.'

'Shut up! Right. Start winding. I've got her weight.'

The boys had pulled me barely two feet off the ground when suddenly I heard a man's voice.

'Oi, you kids, what in God's name are you doing?' I saw three new faces peer into the pit. The one on my right spoke.

'All right, littl'un, you come up now. We're going to haul you up. Get that rope very firmly under your arms now and hold on.'

Al protested that he was quite capable of doing the winching himself. But I was cold now, I didn't care who pulled me up. My teeth were chattering, despite the patch of summer blue sky above. A flurry of earth crumbled off the edge where the rope touched and scattered into the pit. A speck of soil fell into my mouth.

'Ruddy hell, it's a girl.' They were wearing thick indigo cotton overalls. I guessed they must have spotted us from the building site. They must have been doing overtime.

'Hold tight, love, for crying out loud.' As I approached warmer, fresher air the square of now palest blue sky widened into a big screen, out of which two pairs of waving arms and hands reached towards me. One pair grabbed hold of me. They belonged to a short man who I noticed had tears in his eyes. He said I could have been buried alive. It was a phrase I associated with coal-mining accidents. I had seen pictures on the news of weeping relatives waiting at the top of the pit. The man dusted me down and looked at me hard. 'Right, now get off home! And don't ever be so daft as to do anything like that again. I've a good mind to tell your mum and dad. You daft lads. The girl could have been killed.'

My two friends bowed their heads.

'But we only live up there,' I protested. The nearness of home and family seemed like protection.

'And that's where you should get off to. Right now, mind. We're waiting to see you go.' They climbed the hill to watch and wait.

Al noticed the stoat in the jar. 'Well done,' he whispered. 'See yer then.' He had to walk home, because he had spent his bus fare on a cigarette.

'Yeah, see yer, Al,' I said. Then I looked around. 'Stay a bit, Robbie. You don't have to go, do you?'

I looked around to make sure Al had gone.

'Heh, you're crying.'

'I feel sorry for the stoat.'

'Yes,' said Robbie gravely. 'It's so frightened it probably thinks it's going to die.'

I tipped the stoat out on to my hand and stroked the dull brown fur once. It wasn't even pretty. Then I set it down on the grass. For a moment it remained motionless, as if its brain were slow to receive the message from its outer senses, but then it dashed away into the darkness of the forest.

'Let's try on our clothes!'

'Let's!' The soft pinkness of my mum's bedroom reminded me of her skin. I sprawled on the big bed and stared at a different ceiling. I never went into that mysterious room unless it was with her, but I loved it when I got there. I tried out all the matching objects on the dressing-table. There was a chrome-plated hand mirror and a soft hairbrush, a clothes brush and a perfume syphon with a silk-covered rubber squirter. All of these came in a shade of damask rose. I tried the clothes brush on my face and with the hand mirror jiggled about till I could see the back of my neck reflected in the larger mirror. She let me rub cream into my hands, while I sat with my legs dangling on the long linen basket and watched her try on outfits in front of the mirror, which was normally hidden inside the wardrobe door. We seemed to be in her bedroom for hours, as she altered her hair, her shoes, her expression, and her posture, with the occasional cry: 'Do you really think it suits me? I think it's quite old-fashioned. I'll have to get something new.' At the end of a wardrobe session dresses and tops and shoes and belts and hats were all spread out over the bed and the bed already took up most of the space. I didn't know how Dad could find a place for himself.

'Can we look at the photographs?' There was no harm in asking, even if I did risk a burst of temper, depending on her mood. She kept the family photographs in the linen basket, another of the sort-of-secrets in her room. It was a pink-painted wicker chest with a padded cushion top. If you flipped up the top on its hinges you could get easily at what was inside, not bones, but definitely stories from the past.

'If you must.' She was worrying about a skirt length, trying to hold it above her knee and see the effect at the same time.

I spread the photographs over the dressing-table side of the bed and prayed she wouldn't suddenly need the space. Ceri, my dead granny, was a bigger and more confident- looking woman than my mother and there was picture of her striding determinedly across a park in a skirt that came way below her knee. She was born in 1890 and she was a driver during the war. That must have been great, or swell, as Clint Eastwood said in *Rawhide*. That must have been swell. Pity I never really met my granny of the tough breed. She died when I was three.

How different was the snap of my mother! Photographed with her father in a garden, my mum was rather a slight and bewildered child, with bright, narrow little eyes, a small nose, and a small head she carried on one side. Her father – they called him Bertie – looked terribly old beside his youngest daughter, and his expression was tired and far away. His real name was Hubert Luck-Carter and he too was unknown to me. He died before I was born. All I could see was that he was not interested in his daughter and hated the camera. He not only never smiled, but always managed to half-obscure himself from sight, behind a newspaper or book, or another person, or a half-open door.

I shuffled through the other pictures. There were several of Frieda, my mother's elder sister by seven years, but only one of Dorothy, two years older. She was sitting in the same garden as my mother, but lolling in her chair like a fat rag doll. 'Don't *loll*, Lynne-Caroline!' my mother often told me.

'Tell me the story again,' I begged.

For once she did. 'Oh, we were quite grand, we had servants, until Daddy lost his money.'

Somehow I thought she was telling the truth this time. 'But how did he *lose* it?' I wailed. I had visions of Hubert's wealth dropping out of his pocket, of coins rolling along the pavement and down the drain. Or I thought he had put it somewhere and just couldn't remember where, though such an act of forgetting was difficult for me to imagine.

When my mother finally explained it to me she was standing there in a white knee-length slip, and only the way her mouth puckered stopped her resembling a goddess. I was the only child in my class who had heard of the Wall Street Crash, only the way she told the story, how she talked of steel in America, suggested that evil had personally singled out the Luck-Carters. Then Dorothy 'who was never right in the head' was given away to a Home, and then the war came.

My poor, dear mummy. She lay curled sideways on the bed,

on top of the pink bedspread, surrounded by new clothes and old photographs, and spouted tears and moans. I leaned over and stroked her head. That's why she didn't like talking to me. My questions brought on her attacks.

On Saturday morning Dad and I went to the Kardomah for coffee. We had our favourite place to park the car for nothing, where a single building had been bombed, near the Library, and as always it was a little triumph to find it free and to walk then into the centre of town like knowing visitors, like people thoroughly in charge of our lives. Dad wanted me to feel that confidence. Mum wasn't at all like that. She encouraged me to be naughty. The Kardomah building was tall and L-shaped, all decked out in the roasted brown colour of coffee beans matched with bright orange. 'Is it an Indian name, Dad?'

'I don't know, Linka.'

'I thought they drank tea in India.'

He was wearing a wool sports jacket and my favourite shirt of his, made of soft cotton, check on cream. 'Linka, I have to tell you something...' We often went for Saturday morning coffee, but usually after the shopping. Today the shopping wasn't important.

'It's a blend of tea, sir, in answer to the young lady's question. What can I get you?'

'Pot of coffee for one and a strawberry milkshake, please.' He managed a tight smile.

'Yes, Dad?' I pressed.

'Well, I know it's hard for you, Linka, but your mother's a little bit ill.'

'Yes, Dad.'

The Kardomah became a blur, like a room filmed from outside through rain-washed windows. The colours and the hard rectangular shapes dissolved and re-formed themselves. Earth colours and thin black lines of wire, and bursts of flame.

'You're such a show-off,' said Robbie. I showed off at school and he hated it. The journey to school transformed me from his special friend to a person he couldn't own. At the same time something else was happening. I was now eleven and a half and nature was opening my eyes.

Patrick O'Brien wasn't our school gang leader, I was, despite being a girl, but the gang centred on him, because he was bigger and older. He was tall and plump, and, like me, he was always showing off. In his last school he hadn't done all the work so when he joined our class he had to catch up. He lived in a huge house in a much older area than ours, which was definitely posh. He had a whole room with bare boards on the top floor just for his train set, and a garden with a greenhouse and brick outhouse and some old stables where they kept junk. He was a child like the young masters and mistresses of Esper House must have been. What were they like? Well, I only had stories to go by. But I thought of them as boys and girls who shared their days with dogs and ponies and sailed in their own boats on lakes which lapped their gardens. When those rich children's balls went astray they smashed panes in greenhouses and the gardener came to Father to complain. When they played hide-and-seek they searched rooms with unusual names like the pantry and the attic, the cellar and the potting shed. Sometimes their quarry turned up in the nursery and sometimes in the orchard, where the gardener was hard at work. Plums and apples and pears ripened. Mother made pies and jams and packed picnics.

Whenever I was invited to Patrick's house I wondered whether my mum would have been happier there. But actually Patrick was just like us, only his family lived in a big house.

In our lunch-hour we let ourselves in the back way. Bettina, who was very fair and fragile-looking and liked boys, came along too. Suddenly Bettina and I found ourselves locked in the old stables with the junk. The boys disappeared out of sight. There was Patrick and Alan and a boy called Michael, who looked a bit like Clint Eastwood and a bit like my dad. Bettina's friend Danny was also there. I didn't like him, but he was always there. When they eventually opened the door they had flushed faces and were grinning. They were jostling each other and edging forward like people – or horses – getting ready to run a race, or cattle massing to stampede. Clint Eastwood would have said them steers were spooked. A kind of heat came off the boys in our gang, and great merriment.

'It tastes sort of sour!' said Patrick, to which Michael replied, 'Shh! No, not in front of them, they're girls!'

Patrick made a bit of theatre about pulling up his zip, which set them all laughing again. 'You're a girl! You're not supposed to know!' he laughed.

But I want you to know, I understood him to be saying. And so I replied, 'I do though. I saw you through the crack,' and even though the first claim was hazy and the second a downright lie, I kept in with the pack of boys by jostling with them, my energy smashing against theirs. This was what being in our gang was about. Robbie wasn't there because he wasn't rough enough, but I was. Alan was there, but he just smiled a bit and was quiet.

The boys declared they were hungry. Patrick knew that the fanlight in the kitchen was left open when his mother went out. He hoisted up Alan on his shoulders and Alan, very agile, reached in and released the catch below. We climbed in one after the other, over the draining board, and tiptoed about noisily, giggling and shushing each other. Alan helped Bettina and climbed in last. Patrick got out a big tin of biscuits and made a jug of orange squash. We had such a good feast we were ten minutes late back for registration. Since we were allowed out at lunch-times we said the bus had broken down and we had to walk. This excuse was accepted and we worked quietly for the rest of the afternoon.

After that day Michael and I smiled at each other quite a lot and he told me I was a nice girl. When Patrick got wind of our smiling at each other like that he insisted on taking us into his parents' bedroom the very next Saturday morning. His mum was out shopping and we were supposed to be upstairs in the attic playing with the train set. I don't know where his dad was. The double bed was high and well-cushioned. A white candlewick bedspread covered the pillows and eiderdown. Patrick, actually a whole year and a half older than us, suddenly said, 'Here's where you do it...' and went red. His face looked like a balloon about to burst.

The others crowded around in the doorway, but he turned and pushed them away, leaving us together behind the closed door. We stood alone, framed and intimidated by the silence. The room and everything in it seemed immensely alien, until Michael gave me his best Hollywood crinkly smile and we held hands, leaning against the edge of the tall bed. Our five minutes of love ended with a tiny dry kiss. We never spoke about it again.

Miss Rogers was furious about the break-in at Patrick's. I'd never seen anyone so angry. The week before that meeting with the parents she marched into our classroom and called us out in the corridor by name. She said we had no respect for property and had lied and behaved like common thieves. Then we followed her in silence to her room. She walked very fast and her flat shoes squeaked on the linoleum. It was like being given a tour of the school which, as we were often told, had been designed by the famous architect Adrian Bell and had won a prize as a lovely light place to learn in.

We crowded into her room, rather like the boys had tried to crowd into the bedroom where Patrick had taken Michael and me. She had the boys line up on one side and Bettina and me on the other. Then she opened the cupboard, which, as we all knew, contained her canes. There were six of them, sandy-coloured and bendy as whips, like one of the young ash shoots I stripped with my penknife. Patrick farted and for a moment that was all I could think about. Then the poor boys stepped forward in turn, dropped their shorts, bent over and she caned them six times on the back of their bare legs. The tears spurted out of my eyes, hot and uncontrollable, when I saw those red lines appear on their legs. I had never cried so much, not even in the Kardomah, and my head filled with Miss Rogers's words about not giving in to wickedness.

We only managed to talk about it a week later.

'Who told her, Pat?'

'Jones the gardener. He said it was a sin, what we did, you
know, and you girls were to blame.'

I hated gardeners from that moment.

A letter went home saying we girls had encouraged the boys
in sinful acts. I heard my mother laughing, and found the letter
left on the kitchen table for me to read, which is why I was so
surprised she came up to the school to finally 'clear things up'.
Finally we had to apologise to Mr and Mrs O'Brien for
climbing into their house.

My mum and dad were arguing. I could always hear them even
if I was upstairs. The walls in our house were actually as thin
as prefabs, only made of something different. 'Emma, you have
to look after this child. All she ever does is watch television. I
have a job to do and I'm running for selection as the Party
candidate. Be reasonable.'

'It's all so boring, Charlie. You are boring. This little house
is absolutely boring and I think I might kill myself.'

'That's a risk I'll have to take,' he shouted angrily and I
heard the Anglia rev up and reverse too fast out of the drive.
In the kitchen something broke, and there was the sound of
tears. I didn't want to be left alone with her so even though it
was dark I slipped out to the far end of the road, the finished
end, near the Emsworths at number five and far from the
building site, and climbed my favourite tree. I called it the
Watchtower.

''ello, Linka. What you doin' up there like a sleepin' bird?
Don' you wanner come down and look for the fox?'

'What are you doing out so late, Sen?'

He shone his torch on me. 'I could ars you the same

question!' He just kept looking at me and smiling. 'Iss ten o'clock. Come on down, Linka. Sen'll look after yer.'

I pretended to think. 'I'd like to see the fox, Sen, only not tonight. I've, I've ... got homework.' I lied. Miss Rogers never gave us homework. Only Anne and Amy Hill from the private school had homework and they called it prep.

Sen shrugged. 'Don't you get becomin' too clever, Linka. It ain't good for girls.'

'I'm bored.'

'Let's play rangers.'

'We played that yesterday.'

'So what?'

I persuaded Robbie it was good to pedal up and down looking for an animal we could rescue, or for people doing something strange. On other days we played his game, which we called Worldwatchers.

'In the war they had to have messengers to tell the Civil Defence where the bombs had fallen, and where people were in trouble. Bombs made huge craters like that pit where we were looking for the stoats. And people couldn't get out, or got buried alive, so they had to have people like us riding up and down and watching out. And they had to watch out for German spies.'

It was good. I should have thought of it.

Through the front window of number fourteen we saw the Polish man sitting in one of two brown chairs, with a book on his knee, but looking straight ahead. 'What's he doing? Thinking about Poland?'

'He's listening to music. Look! He's got a record-player.' We passed the pillar box and turned at the Watchtower tree to

come back and have another look. First we cycled fast, then we
meandered, practising wiggling our front wheels and
balancing. That too was part of the game. Technique.

'There's your dad going home.' Dad was too preoccupied to
notice us a couple of hundred yards away.

We freewheeled down to number twenty-three where Mrs
Hill was weeding the garden. We were collecting information
where we could. What we mostly learned, from creeping under
our neighbours' windows and peering through their
letterboxes, was that human beings lead regular lives. At the
same time every day Susan Birkett put Timmy down for a sleep,
after lunch, and relaxed with a cup of tea and a cigarette. She
was plump and often tired. As for the Polish man, every day at
four o'clock, before he went to work, he did some keep-fit
exercises in his back garden.

'We're practising for the next war.'

Robbie's eyes bulged. 'Who are we going to fight?'

'The Russians of course, and the Communists.'

'The Polish man?'

'No, stupid. He's not Communist.'

'He might be. You don't know, Linka.' Communism was
another word we heard a lot and didn't quite know what it
meant.

We passed Mrs Hill's again, and on the other side number
twenty-two, where Sheena and Mike lived behind a buttercup
yellow front door.

Unaware of our approach, someone crossed the road.
Robbie rang his bell.

Mrs Emsworth turned, startled, before smiling at him.
'Come on, Macnamara, mind the bicycles.'

Robbie pinged in thanks and the dog yapped. We pedalled right up to the building site until the sandy track petered out and then turned to face the road again.

'There's your dad going out again.'

The Anglia reversed into the road. The brake lights came on. From behind, with its chrome fins, it looked like a space rocket facing the wrong way.

'Come on, I've got an idea.'

We passed between our back door and the garage, and entered the back garden on all fours. The best view would have been from the ash trees looking straight into the French windows, but we had no cover, so again, we had to crawl under the next window. We had to be quiet for she had all the windows open. It wasn't summer yet, but there she was, wearing her favourite summer dress, white, fitted at the waist and then flared to the knee, with big black polka dots. She was dancing. In fact, she was switching the wireless on and off, using the knob as her jiving partner. She twirled with a pillow and kissed it. Then she lay on the ground and hugged it.

'Your kind father does everything for your mother,' said Marjorie Hill, while Anne and Amy and I ate homemade cake and scones, and eyed each other. 'Is she an invalid, Linka?'

'Whatever gives you that idea, Mrs Hill?'

'She very rarely comes out.'

I looked round the Hills' sitting room. There were bookshelves and newspapers but everything was a sort of pale brown colour and there wasn't a television. The pictures on the walls were cut out from magazines. Mum wouldn't have liked to live there.

'She's...' I sought desperately for a word. 'She's bored. There aren't enough things to interest her in the whole world.'

Mrs Hill leaned forward, half-smiling, silently urging me to come closer to the right answer.

'She wants to be a free woman. To be modern,' I said finally.

Mrs Hill looked offended, as if I'd said a rude word. 'Let's have a quiz! Anne, get some pencils and scrap paper from my desk. You're a clever girl, Linka. You're never bored, are you?' *From today Linka Beecham will sit on her own.* Off we went.

'What was the name of the British Prime Minister during the war?'

'What is the capital of Russia?'

'What is the name of the island off the south of Australia?'

'Who said: "Dr Livingstone, I presume?"'

I got the name of the Prime Minister and the year of the Battle of Britain. But finally I failed.

'Don't you know French for cat, Linka?'

'We don't do French at school.'

'But your mother should teach you. Or doesn't she know French herself?'

I pushed my chair back from Mrs Hill's horrible table. 'I prefer to play outside than learn silly French or do quizzes!' I blurted. 'It's much more fun.'

'Dear me, Linka, there's no need to get quite so cross. It's only a bit of fun.'

It isn't, it isn't. You're trying to hurt me.

Little Amy stared, but Anne Hill gave me a nice look I understood. It wasn't her fault she had such a mother.

'Right, come on, I'm not staying here while they have one of their nasty Labour Party meetings in my kitchen. We'll go to the pictures.'

'What does "A" mean?' I whispered, as we climbed up the carpeted stairs of the Gaumont. It was quite a grand place, with marble and bright lights and soft furnishings everywhere.

'It means you're twelve.' She winked. 'Two in the stalls please, halfway back.'

'Golly, Mum, are you sure I—?'

'Yes, shh now.' This was her dream. This was what she wanted.

The film showed people at an airport, on an aeroplane and then drinking cocktails in Monte Carlo, where there was a casino. We had to move once because a man and woman in the row in front were kissing and Mum said she couldn't bear that. The usherette came and shone her torch inquiringly to which Mum replied she didn't know the Gestapo were now running Brightsea cinema. But finally she settled. 'Technicolor. I like that.'

Poor Mummy. Perhaps if she'd been evacuated to Monte Carlo it would have been all right. The characters in the film were obviously rich, dressed in very smart clothes and jewellery and riding around in big open cars. Next time Robbie said we were rich I would tell him that was rubbish. He'd never seen what real rich people were like. Now I was bored. Mrs Hill was right. It didn't happen to me often. I waited for something exciting to happen, but it didn't. So I watched my mum instead. This was my mum, to whom, during the war, when she was a child like I was now, someone called Mildred Pickles had not been kind. Mildred had a son called Ralph and a daughter called Margot. They got warm rooms and nice food while my mum had to sit alone and eat her crusts. So she said. Now she was dreaming of being magicked away to Monte Carlo. Her eyes blinked, and occasionally she wiped them with a handkerchief. Her lips mouthed words. She even seemed to lean forwards into the screen, as if she wanted to live amongst those people. I had the idea to kiss her, but I was afraid. And so we stayed for nearly two hours.

Finally we stood up for the national anthem. I always liked that moment when everyone behaved properly. It was like school. I felt I knew where I was and what was going to happen next. I even hummed a bit of 'Praise My Soul the King of Heaven' to prolong the good moment. Then we went out into the fresh air. She was standing stiffly beside me, with her face directed into the far distance, staring at nothing in particular.

'We could go away, Lynne-Caroline. Would you like that?'

'What about Dad?'

'He's wrapped up in his politics.'

'But he needs someone to look after him,' I protested, and, not knowing where my words came from, added, 'He can't eat fish and chips or have a pie down at the Labour Party all the time.'

On the other hand a voice in my head reminded me that my mum was 'not a slave to any man or any child'. She couldn't be, could she? She was getting ready to run away to the Promised Land.

'One of us has to go away,' she said, not directly to me. 'We can't go on like this. Only we don't have any money.'

'Maybe we could go to Poland,' I replied.

'Linka, don't be ridiculous.'

'To see Frieda in London then.'

'That's more like it.'

From that tree where I liked to sit and contemplate Esper Road, the one we called the Watchtower, I could see a long scar running down the field. The builders had been going to lay pipes there but changed their minds and now the ditch was mostly overgrown and half-collapsed, but if you looked you could still find it.

I fixed a rendezvous with Robbie for six o'clock.

I set off a bit before.

Swinging through the ash trees at the end of our garden, I slipped down the other side and took a few paces until I could sit in long grass. My eye wandered a bit, but then settled on where the fields met the forest. The forest and fields seemed to me like two people reaching out towards each other. I enjoyed that thought.

Then Robbie joined me and we picked our way down the ditch until we came to a section about four feet deep. That would do. I had a plan to build a new den. My eyes roamed upwards towards the building site. 'Come on.' He hung back. 'Robbie, the builders have gone home. They knock off at four. Normally. We're not going to get caught. We'll just take something they don't need.'

'I don't like it, Linka, it's stealing.'

'In that case I'm going without you.'

After a few minutes Robbie followed.

Out of hours there were all sorts of things to play on around the new houses. We ran across the tinkling stacks of bricks, kicked in the mounds of sand, thundered across gang-planks

and pressed our noses to new windows. My eye caught a piece
of corrugated iron, like the roof of a prefab.

'Now come and help me carry it.' Taking hold either side, we
dragged the rough, uneven sheet of metal from the slope
beneath the unfinished houses and back towards the trench.
Over the bumps in the ground the sharp corner dug into my
palm and made it bleed. Blood made me think I was a heroine
and doing the right thing.

'Put it across so it makes a roof. That's it.' I stood on the
metal. It was firm and almost level. 'Now, I'll just try it inside.'
I jumped down and sat cross-legged on the rough earth and
weed-covered floor of the ditch, with the iron panel about a
foot above my head. The iron was heavy and cast its shadow
like the spread wing of a huge crow, but it made a den, for now
the ditch had become like a cave with a patch of fading light at
each end, and the ground sloping gently downwards.

'What will you do for end bits?'

'Nothing. It's fine. Come and try.' *From today Linka
Beecham will sit on her own.*

'In the war they were called Anderson shelters,' Robbie
pontificated. 'People had them in their back gardens.'

'And did refugees stay in them? Mr Braunschweig's a
refugee.'

'That's different.'

'Come on, we need to camouflage it otherwise people will
bomb it.' We tore up grass and bracken and threw it over the
roof of my shelter. I tried to imagine my mum there and threw
some more dried grass inside to make it more comfortable. I
couldn't do anything about the approaching darkness.

'I'm going to stay out tonight to try it.'

In the voice of his father and mother, when they worried about him, Robbie asked, 'You'll be all right then, Linka?'

'Of course I'll be all right. Tell you about it tomorrow.'

'See you then.' And I watched his thin little legs battle their way through the overgrown stalks of grass that barred his path uphill and home.

I wasn't frightened. As I listened to the birds, and watched through the stalks of crisp bracken for any approaching wolves, I marvelled at the sounds around me. I heard a chorale to which my memory contributed many tunes and sounds. People were talking on wirelesses, and at Dad's meetings (where I sometimes went and fell asleep on two chairs at the side of the room), and talking different languages like the French Mrs Hill knew and the German Dad remembered from the war (*Hugo's Improve Your German*, with a blue-grey paper cover, priced 2/6d). Then there were the languages I could read on my stamps. Deutsche Reichspost. CCCP (which I confused with the five rings of the Olympic Games). *Bonjour. Le chien. Guten Tag. Ich heisse Linka.*

'Why are you learning German again, Dad?' I would ask.

'Because the war is over, sweetheart. To show it need never happen again if we understand each other.'

One night the wireless said, '*Hier ist der Sender Freies Berlin.*' He was testing himself.

No, I wasn't frightened. There was the song of nature, of trees and grass. If you stay out at night you can hear things growing, and little animals rustling everywhere. The earth has its own language. The forest called to me and I signalled back, three long hoots. I poked my head out again about half an hour after nightfall. The bushes were alive like unsleeping cats, with open eyes and ears, then suddenly it was just as if the whole world had sunk beneath bedclothes. Everything shut down. A late bird screeched and flew over. Only the last two houses of presently inhabited Esper Road, those of the Pandraneths and the Hills, rose distantly above the horizon and showed their lights.

The next thing I heard voices.

'Linka's in her new den, Mr Beecham.'

'Where? Show me, Robbie, show me! It's so dark out here.'

I felt myself blush. I had borrowed the battery out of Dad's torch.

'She's camouflaged it, of course.' Robbie sounded impressed and it was fun that he couldn't quite remember where I was.

'What was that?' asked Dad. 'Hoot again.'

'Nothing,' Robbie said. 'Unless it was a real owl.' And he laughed nervously, which made me want to laugh.

'You must remember, for heaven's sake. You were here only a few hours ago. I'll have to call the police in a minute.'

Robbie was enjoying being the lynchpin of the search operation. His voice sounded animated and self-important. 'If we go down to the tree stump, sir, I can probably find my way from there.'

Then he was out of earshot and I could only picture him climbing up the dinosaur and surveying our territory and sniffing the wind and examining the stars. He was the captain, the leader of the expedition, with the right to cry, 'Yes! I think I know the place, sir. Follow me.' I heard the tindery bracken snap under their feet. Those tall stalks the colour of dried blood were like a line of matchstick sentries guarding me in my stronghold. Dad overtook Robbie to run the last few yards. He approached nearer and nearer and sounded breathless.

'Help me. Take the far corner. One two three, lift!'
Something heavy landed in the grass and the sky was torn from
above my head. The loose grass slid off and the shocked metal
lay resonating. Dad picked me up from where I had been
crouching. His hands were shaking.

'Dad?' I grinned and stretched, and put my arms round him.
'*Guten Tag, ich heisse Linka!*'

He picked me up and carried me home.

'What were you thinking of?' he murmured.

'In case the war comes. In case I have to look after myself.
Sometimes in war children lose their parents and they have to
survive on their own.'

'You'd better get off home now, son. Say goodnight to your
mum for me. We'll see you in from here.' Dad and I watched, in
the light of the orange street lamps, as Robbie ostentatiously
rang at his own front door bell. Robbie had done his work as a
mountain ranger and saved his friend the lost girl. He was a
hero. His mother Deirdre, who made fridges and washing
machines, waved and shut the door.

'Where's Mum?' I wanted to reassure myself I had a better
mother than Mrs Evans, who was dowdy. But mine wasn't
there.

'She must be still at Susan Birkett's.' Dad made me a milky
drink and we sat for a while and watched the boxing, then we
turned out the lights and went to bed. I looked at my watch
when I heard her come in, having forced myself to stay awake.
It was midnight, and my heart started banging.

'I thought you weren't coming.'

Alan was still in his short grey school trousers, and his

mustard pullover tied around his waist. I brought Penguins and we had tea in the fields. I wanted to ask him back, but it was awkward with my mum not wanting to be a slave to anyone.

'How's your mum?'

'My mum?'

'Yes.'

'She's OK. Why d'you ask?'

'My mum says your mum wants a boyfriend. Everyone knows that in the whole of Brightsea. She goes out on her own.'

I pictured her then, dressing up and going out. Leaving home. Coming under the eye of strangers. In the new yellow dress and jacket perhaps, with the black hat. Or she had some slim navy trousers, which she liked to wear with a bright shirt; great big whirls of red and green and brown on a white background.

'But my dad's her boyfriend, isn't he?'

'I don't know.'

'But he must be. He's her husband. Are your mum and dad friends?'

'I'll say.'

'But not posh.'

'My dad's a roundsman, Linka.'

'What's Patrick's dad?'

'An accountant.'

'What's that?'

Neither of us knew. I lay on my back and examined the sky.

'Linka, your mum, does she do sex?'

'What's that?'

'A man puts his willy up the lady. It's in all the films.'

'Liar!'

'Honest. You just have to see an X film. X is dirty. Shall I tell you?'

'No!' I was happy for a moment lying in that field, looking at the sky.

'Linka! You're always doing your thinking. Why can't you be like the rest of us?'

We lay next to each other in silence.

'She was evacuated. Don't you know? It means sent away in the war to stay with people you don't know, who are nasty to you. And then if you have a bad life it makes you dream.'

I remembered Mum's face from the cinema, when she wanted to climb into a story and couldn't bear for it to be over. That sort of going out didn't work.

Alan was propped on one side with a blade of grass flopping out of his mouth. He looked so kind and always sounded both young and old. He spoke with his parents' voices and had their wisdom, their prejudices, their words, yet was also a boy. 'Linka, do you know how babies are made? Let me tell you!'

'No, Al, no, just shut up!' I leapt on him and knelt on his arms and tried to bang his head against the ground. But there was too much grass for that to hurt, so I pushed my hands against his. My toecaps scrabbled to get a hold in the slippery grass. He was at a disadvantage, underneath, trying to keep his white arms straight. The effort was costing me all the strength I had. Yet at the same time it was different from fighting with Robbie. I had to force myself not to stop fighting and just enjoy it. 'Give in!' Alan bucked his body beneath me but I sat tight, and he conceded.

'Yeah, I give in!'

I relaxed, he tipped me off and we rolled down the hill laughing.

'Linka, did you hear what I said? I said your mother's a bit ill.'

A bit ill? I remembered her dancing with the pillow. So what? She liked dancing. Our neighbour Mrs Girton could stare all she liked, as I had told her when she cornered me back in February and asked me why all the windows were open and the wireless blaring.

'A bird flew in,' I said. 'They often do. We put the music on loud and open all the windows to get the birds to fly out.'

'Will she get better, Dad?' I saw my ugly, boyish reflection in the chrome coffeepot in the Kardomah.

'Let's hope so.'

'Don't *you* hope so, Dad?' He didn't answer. I added, 'Maybe God can make her better.'

That made him furious. Only stupid people believed in God.

'Like Miss Rogers, Dad?'

Someone had to promise something better. We heard a lot about God at school, and He didn't seem to me bad at all, with his many mansions and his terrible punishments. God knew everything, created everything, understood everything, made it good.

I went down again into the fields with Alan, this time as far as the forest clearing where Sen had come to see me and Robbie. The stump and the plank were still there, but the green plants and leaves had grown so much that the spot was completely enclosed. It was a warm May evening.

'Shall we look at each other, Linka? You know.'

I did. I took my wellingtons off, and my trousers, and my white socks and navy school pants and my T-shirt, and I stood there naked with my feet cushioned by the warm felty floor of pine needles. Our bodies were white and Alan had no hair, just a willy. And I could see his ribs. The fresh air played on my skin.

He reached out his hand.

No!

'Don't be scared, Linka. You've got tits. That's nice.'

I looked at him for a while. 'You're so lucky being a boy.'

He walked over to his schoolbag and when he crouched down to undo it he was like a wild beast in the forest. The way his legs folded into his body was beautiful.

He took out the familiar punctured jam jar. 'Look, I've brought you another stoat. A really beautiful one this time. Let's lie down in the grass out there and be with the stoat. You can let it go afterwards if you want.'

'Someone might come.'

'No one will come.'

No one did, and the stoat tickled us with his legs and fur.

I asked Al to come up to the building site with me. 'Meet you by the sand patch at seven.'

The evenings were really light now, which gave us lots of time but meant we could be seen. We went as late as we could. Al was allowed to come home at 8 p.m. Mrs Robertson wasn't as strict as Deirdre Evans.

White dust and an uncanny stillness had settled everywhere. The evening was such a contrast with the busy day. We trampled a pile of bright orange sand. Then I picked up a long thin baton of wood to use as a swordstick. We moved as if from ride to ride in a fairground. The brick stack was not as good as it looked, because it wobbled like a cakewalk, and when the bricks fell they cut our legs and bruised our feet in plimsolls. For once I would have needed my wellingtons, but it was now June, and my mother had decided there was no more mud to turn her into a slave and so now I should absolutely wear plimsolls. No choice about it. Under my thinly clad feet I liked the tinkling sound new bricks made. The light, high notes somehow belonged in a fairy story. Their wobble let me imagine we were at sea in a storm, or, because of the danger, that we were darting over rooftops. They were the music to my film. Alan and I were like my mother trying on new outfits, but clothes were nothing compared with the lives and adventures we ran through on a warm evening deserted of people. This building site after hours, this wonderful playground, was the whole world and the beginning and end of time. It reminded me of something I liked hearing in assembly – 'world without end'. God's world. It was pinkish grey and had been left unfinished. As everyone knew, God had been disturbed on the sixth day of his labours, and sometimes you could feel the gaps. Sometimes you felt there wasn't anything there, or that it was all uncertain, just plans and shadows and imaginings, and brick stacks and houses without doors and windows without glass. Numbers twenty-seven to fifty-two in Esper Road were unfinished. Who would live in these houses? How would they live in them? And what then would the houses become? We too, we children, could become anything, live anywhere, or vanish.

We chose the still numberless house, which had all its walls, and wooden roof rafters in place, but no glass panes in the windows and only swathes of polythene to keep it dry. There was a doorless doorway, but we passed through a window just because that wouldn't always be possible. The house would start to become ordinary once the glaziers came.

'That's where they'll put the cooker.' We knew the difference between the very thick, slightly flattened black cables that served a heavy-duty appliance, and the thinner wires that would be hidden behind the various plug sockets for the iron and the wireless and the television. 'What will they cook? What's your favourite meal, Linka?'

'Mmm. Beefburger, chips and peas.' We rubbed our tummies and smacked our lips. Al preferred instant mashed potato with salad cream. We staked out the cooking and dining habits of our possible near future. I picked up some loose nails and put them in my pocket.

'Come on, let's explore upstairs.' It was strange. I thought of our explorations as a journey into the future but the flesh-coloured plaster everywhere had a mouldy, damp smell. The unpainted window frames were also a sort of pink, flesh-like colour. We wanted to touch everything around us as if for the first time. The newly sanded wood around the doorways felt like silk, while putty was mysterious stuff. Wet and dry, smooth and crumbly, alive and dead, who could describe it? What *was* it? Then again, if, outside, under polythene wrappings, you thrust your hand into one of the double-walled brown paper sacks you could let grey cement powder run through your fingers. You expected it to be like flour, only it stung your skin, and penetrated every crevice on the back of your hand. When you clapped your hands to drive out the feeling of being unclean you couldn't get it off and the dust made you cough.

'Can your dad build things?'

'He's promised my mum to do a path. Where the grass is at our front.'

'My dad can do concrete. I've seen him do that. You just get water and mix it and pour it in between planks. Then you have to stop the cats and birds and dogs coming, or they leave their footprints. It's really funny. Inside our garage you can see a birdprint when the car's not there. And a place where I dipped my finger and wrote L.'

Now Alan and I were walking about bedrooms without wallpaper, or paint, or carpets, our feet sounding hard against the clean, blond boards. These rooms were the barest shelters, and the only thing we could furnish them with was sound.

'Here's where the mum and dad's bed would go, in the biggest room.' I traced the shape by walking around the perimeter of an imagined bed, and then climbed inside it, on to boards scattered with chiselled shavings like Bettina's blonde curls. I sat with my back against the wall. Alan came and sat beside me. We faced the window on to what one day would be the garden.

'Shh a minute, I want to feel how completely silent it is.'

It wasn't. A spattering of summer rain, the moist, laden, grey in the pink sky, hit the polythene above our heads, but the evening outside was still, and its pinkness enhanced the fleshliness of the unfinished house into which we had stolen.

During the day this site was furious with activity. Pile-drivers stamped and drills whined. Another contraption sounded like a machine-gun in slow motion, and there would be the occasional human shout. For the extended road mechanical diggers on caterpillar tracks worked the old overgrown field,

ploughing and seesawing their way through the red soil like
tanks in the war. If the men were working on the roof of a
single old building that had to be demolished – a last outpost
belonging to Esper House perhaps – I could see rocks hurtling
down tin funnel pipes, scraping the sides, jostling and colliding
with each other, and I imagined a landslide. But now it was
completely still.

'We're a mum and dad.'

'We're a couple.'

We hugged our way into the shadow of a possible future.

Then it was half-term and both Robbie and Alan were away.
The day it rained I waited impatiently for TV to start. The test
card, with a noise like an air raid siren, was all that was on till
four. Our TV was a box about three feet tall with doors like a
cupboard. Most of the box was a speaker covered with a fine
mesh like the front of the wireless. The glass part looked like
the very thick glasses of a boy at school. It was like looking into
another eye, because there was a kind of pupil in the centre, but
the whole was grey and watery and without character until you
switched on. As 'the set' 'warmed up' a light appeared. I
thought of God. His first thought of Creation warmed up like
this. I knelt or lay in front of that box, staring into God's
thoughts, sharing them. I didn't feel alone. From God I moved
to battles. I saw a programme about how they used to build
castles with stones cemented together with animal blood and
mud, and defended themselves by throwing stones and boiling
water on their attackers; and how they used pigs' guts,
stretched out and dried, for windows before they had glass. I
marvelled at the uses of blood. Later, in a battle with nature, I

watched Clint Eastwood drive the cattle from one State to the next, through wind and rain and dust.

'Dad, how d'you get money?'

'You know that. You get a job.'

'And how do you get lots of money?'

He sighed. 'That's a different question. In my view people are rich because other people are poor. No one should have lots of money, then everyone would have enough.' He came back a few moments later. 'Well, you know, it's a point of view. It's what I thought when I was young, when my mother was poor. Not everyone thinks that. My boss in Germany after the war, for instance, would have said that without some people being very rich there could be no help for those at a disadvantage. Major-General Bernard Richards. We called him the Head Man.' Dad spoke with warmth.

We drove into town in the Anglia. I loved that car with its big chrome tail fins, like something out of an American film. It was a swell car.

'I'd like to live in America.'

'You've been watching too many cowboy films.'

'America's a swell place.'

The Civic centre of Brightsea stood white and lifeless as a bleached bone. I couldn't make sense of it. We drove round the empty space like the Queen in her carriage. We left again and parked on the old bomb site. But the morning was mine, because Frieda had sent me ten shillings.

We made for Woolworths. Behind the red and gold signboard, which ran across the front like a banner, Woolworths had big front windows, bare floorboards and a café at the far end, divided from the shop by a chrome barrier. In the middle of the store, on one 'island', I weighed a key ring in pink plastic in my hand. It had a tiny torch at one end. A set of pens in a plastic wallet caught my attention, but it wasn't what a builder needed. Dad loitered with his hands in his pockets. He tried to get some wax out of his ear and suggested I shouldn't buy Japanese rubbish. I bought a packet of sandcastle flags, with the elongated lions of the red ensign stretched across a yellow field on top, and a tape measure.

In the Sports and Camping shop I asked after 'any sort of signalling equipment'. I examined a small paraffin lamp. The smallest was all I could afford, but it would do. 'At least it's not Japanese rubbish.'

The man behind the counter, much older than Dad, replied, 'The Japanese, sir! What a cruel people. Still, times move on, don't they? Got what you want, young lady? Good morning to you.'

'What about the Japanese?'

'Another day, Linka.'

'Can we go to the Scout shop?'

'We'll have to walk.' It was away from the centre, almost in the park.

'Oh swell, Dad, thanks. Race you!'

The floors in that unusual shop were bare board and the air smelt of leather. The counters displayed knives and the niches on the wall had stocks of rope. Even Dad browsed.

'Look, Linka, here's the telephone number. They meet on Tuesdays. Why don't you join?'

'Because they won't let me be a Scout, Dad,' I grinned. 'It's no use pleading.'

'Linka! I meant the Girl Guides.'

'Indeed!' The man in charge joined in. 'You could be a Girl Guide, young lady.'

'And do my duty to God and the Queen.' Anne Hill told me the promises. But I wanted to be a Scout. And I didn't want the adults closing in on me. They always did that. When there was more than one, even though they were complete strangers, all the adults around me formed a chorus. Do this. Don't do that. I found a book, *Manual of Scouting*, with a Foreword by J.H. Wilson, and spent the rest of my money on it.

'Good heavens,' said Dad, looking at the Foreword.

'One and the same, sir. Politics and early responsibility. Though Wilson's not my man. Would you care to make a donation to the Baden-Powell Memorial fund?'

'*I* would like to,' I interjected. Baden-Powell seemed like my kind of person. I dropped sixpence into the tin, while Dad and the man talked about Harold Wilson, nuclear deterrents and America, of which Britain was destined to become the fifty-first state. I still needed a knife. The one I wanted had a brown handle, which was translucent like a jewel. My soul entered that polished stone like into another eye and got lost in its depths. The steel blade was superb. The whole nestled in a leather sheath. Dad saw what I wanted him to see, my longing.

'Here's ten shillings, Linka. Think of it as an early birthday present. But don't tell your mother.'

'Oh, Dad, swell!' The package was made up, polite words were exchanged, and finally the door bell rang, marking our exit.

There was a rat in Esper Road. I spotted him because I was hanging around on my own with nothing special to do. He was a huge dark-grey creature, the colour of wet concrete, twitching and sniffing, sitting in the front drain at number fourteen. Dad rounded up Bob Birkett, who happened to be home, and Mike. Dad was armed with a huge garden spade. Bob carried a fork over his shoulder. Mike brandished a wrench. I felt sorry for the rat and threw a stone at the drainpipe.

'Linka, oh, for heaven's sake! We nearly had him.'

'Sorry, Dad, I thought I might distract his attention while you closed in on him. It's best not to know when you're going to be killed.'

The posse fanned out across the neighbouring front gardens, while Dad knocked on the door, with me just behind. 'Mr Braunschweig!' Dad called.

The Polish man had music playing. Not my mother's kind but what we listened to at school. I knew the names of Mozart and Holst, but perhaps it wasn't either of them.

'Pleass, pleass,' he said, stepping out of his front door in his socks and showing the way round the outside of his house. Dad went through into the back garden and I followed.

The sides of the heaving creature made me think of the pair of bellows Frieda used to light her coal fire. As Dad lifted his spade the Polish man pulled me away. 'You don't want to watch that, Linka, come inside.'

He took me into his kitchen and gave me a drink and a biscuit. But then such a squealing came from the garden that I was unable to touch a drop or a crumb.

He peered out of the French windows, which looked on to a mess of brambles and dandelions fringed by hawthorn. 'Can you put the music on again?' I asked. I felt shy. 'Is the rat there? Is there blood?'

He ran his hands over his face. 'How I hate death. Any death. I don't like seeing anything killed.'

'People kill other people in wars. Nasty men kill little girls, Mum said.' The sweet music played on. I deliberated. My dad surely wasn't a potential killer of men. 'Mr Brunshwig, it's different. A rat's vermin. It's dangerous. It spreads diseases.'

'Vermin, eh? You even have a special word. How I like this country! It's admirable. Rats are dangerous. No doubt, no doubt.'

Our neighbour's voice made something new out of the language familiar to me. Those 'ou' sounds, for instance, in which the o and the u separated, turned 'doubt' into a long, long word. The end even disappeared! Funny. I tried it. He and I made faces at each other. 'What's it like being Polish, Mr Brunshwig?'

'No one can pronounce your name! Listen, Linka. Braunschweig. Brown Shw-eye-g. Say it for me! Good. No, I'll tell you what's good about being Polish in England. You can be a stranger. No one knows about you. No one knows where you come from. And no one asks. See how it is here in Esper Road. They don't notice me because they don't want me to notice them. That way we can all be polite and stick to our private lives. But I'll show you where I come from, shall I?' And he got out a map and showed me where Poland was. To the right of Germany, sorry Miss Rogers, I mean to the east. He told me about the war. Germans and Russians and Poles all fighting each other for the same land. 'You can't imagine that in your peaceful Brightsea.'

Could I not imagine it? His room was bare except for some books piled on the floor and a table and a couple of chairs.

'Which side were you on?'

'None. None. But look . . .' And from inside a book cover he took a small black and white photograph of himself in the Polish army, wearing a uniform with a peaked cap. He was a military doctor. After the Germans arrived, he continued his work underground.

'Underground?'

'In secret.'

'Linka, Linka!' I heard Dad calling through the still open front door. Mr Braunschweig said they must have cleared up their mess.

'Coming, Dad.' I stood up. 'I like to visit you, Mr Brunshwig, even though your house is so empty.'

'Brown Shw-eye-g! But my name is Henryk. Say it! You must come again, Linka. May I call you Linka? You will come and we'll visit Poland together. In our minds, of course.'

'Our Polish friend couldn't rub two sticks together to save his life!' George Woolacott said. 'I've never seen such a mess. What a waste of a nice house.'

The incident of the rat revealed to Esper Road that the owner of number fourteen was not interested in filling it with furniture, or digging his garden, or making anything look nice. 'Our Polish friend' had failed to build a wall, back and front, dividing his house and garden from Mr Woolacott's. He didn't have a gate. His paintwork still wore the pink colour of the builders' undercoat. And his allotted patches of earth back and front were a jungle. Mr Henryk Braunschweig lived at number fourteen Esper Road, but you had to count your way along the road to know that. That disturbed me. No one should lose Henryk Braunschweig in that careless way in which grown-ups lost things. Regretting that I had not bought the pen set in Woolworths, which would have given me the luxury of several colours, I took a pencil and drew a map of Esper Road, with all the numbers and the names of the people, and handed it to the postman. 'His name is Mr Brown Shw-eye-g and he doesn't have a number outside.'

'So that's how you say it, is it? He could always buy one,' replied the postman, folding my map, putting it in his breast pocket. He tapped it to show it was safe underneath the flap and button. 'But thank you, young lady, very thoughtful.'

'In the war they didn't have maps, they burned them all, in case the Germans invaded, isn't that right, Postman?'

'I promise you, Miss, I'll destroy your map if I see a German coming. I'll eat it.' That made me laugh. I liked the postman. I admired his uniform. I liked people in uniforms, like Scouts and policemen, and AA men, and postmen.

I turned up at Henryk's with Dad's garden spade.

'You want to do that now?'

'We could plant something.' I wanted to make people in Esper Road like 'our Polish friend'.

'It's a lot of work.'

'Let's go in then and you show me where Warsaw is.'

'There's not much left of it now, mind. A German leaving present.'

'I speak some German.'

'You do?'

'*Guten Tag. Ich heisse Linka.*'

'Bravo.'

From the map nothing was imaginable. 'Did you live there, in that street, underground?'

'I came up for fresh air from time to time!'

'Say something to me in Polish!'

The tall foreign man with the ragged blue shirt – I could see the white bits coming through at his collar – went over to another of his books and turned the pages. Then he read something: '*Wędrowiec, na istnienie spojrzawszy z ukosa / Wszedł na cmentarz: śmierć, trawa, niepamięć i rosa.*'

The kitchen chair he had brought into the bare sitting room for me was terribly hard, but not so hard as those sounds.

'How do you like that? It's the beginning of a poem.'

I didn't know whether I liked it. But I had that feeling of being sucked into another world, as I was by the deep, cold television screen and the gleaming handle of the sheath knife and the plunge into darkness where the fields gave way to the forest.

'Say it for me again.'

'I'll write it down.'

Then suddenly my mother was there, in Henryk's front garden! Dad and Mr Woolacott had just finished putting up four fence panels on Mr Woolacott's side to divide the two houses, and had summoned Henryk to come and admire them, when my mother came over and joined us in what should have been the front garden.

'You could put some shingle down to keep the front tidy,' ventured George Woolacott acidly.

'Then it would look like the bottom of a birt cage! And I am not a birt.'

Rah, rah, go on Henryk!

Mum must have been watching out of the kitchen window.

She asked the men how they were getting on, something she never normally asked my dad, then she turned to Henryk. 'You're like me. You can't really be bothered to make all this effort. Still, it looks nice. You can't complain.'

He smiled a different smile, from some part of him that had been buried. He didn't smile at me like that, even though he was my friend.

Mum went away to see Frieda, so Dad saw me off to school every morning and left for work later. In the afternoon I picked up the key from the Birketts and was supposed to let myself in. But I spent the time with Henryk. He worked night shifts as an ambulance man, so I could find him at home in the late afternoon.

'Poland and Great Britain were on the same side in the war. The Poles were on the British side against Germany, but that doesn't make me a fighter, Linka. Also, there is something I must tell you about myself. I come in two halves – half-German, half-Polish.'

'Half-German!'

'*Jawohl. Ich heisse Heinrich.*'

'Henryk, don't you *really* mind living in a country where no one understands your words?'

'Not much. It's like living behind a wall, in a pleasant shelter from the wind. Can you imagine?'

'So you like it here in England, in Brightsea! But you don't like housework and gardening?'

He laughed. 'I'm lazy.'

'But you listen to music.'

'I love music.'

'I like music in assembly.' I sang a few bars of 'Praise My Soul the King of Heaven' to demonstrate. 'And when the birds sing. But the best thing about music in nature is silence. That's what I like about Polish.'

'Polish is silent?'

'It's just sounds and I don't know what they mean but I like them around me.'

'You're a young refugee from civilization, Linka!'

'But Henryk you're a refugee, so that makes us the same. Doesn't it? Just a bit?'

'I ran away, Linka, that's all. Don't think I'm a hero. It was ten years after the war. I got the chance to stay on a train and I did. I arrived here and took myself to the nearest police station.'

But Miss Rogers insisted we read about brave people who did good things, like Florence Nightingale and Albert Schweitzer, and Marie Curie and the missionaries to the dark tribes of Africa, and so we were primed to be on the lookout for good people. Henryk Braunschweig seemed to me better than any of them.

'I didn't even run away from war. I ran away from peace. I didn't like the world that grew up around me out of the ruins of the war. It meant more fighting and killing, and more putting people in prison. The whole country was becoming a kind of prison. That was when I left. When you were five years old. I am like a funny shaped piece of wood washed up on Brightsea beach. I don't really fit but this is where I have ended up.'

'We could put you on the nature table. I've got a cat's head I found.'

We went to explore his house. I had never been upstairs. 'Who's this?' There were photographs in a frame, standing on a chair beside his bed. The other two bedrooms were empty, with bare boards.

'My family. I left them behind.'

'Who do you write letters to then? I see you take a letter to the box every Sunday.'

'Linka, you've been spying on me!'

'Only a little.'

'I write to an old teacher of mine.'

'That's where you get the stamps?'

'No I buy them. She doesn't write back.'

'Henryk, do you believe in God?' I ambushed him by the pillar box.

'No, Linka. But that doesn't mean it's not good that you do. We can be different and still like each other. Now, are you rushing somewhere? No? Then come up to the top of the road and tell me what you see. I bet it's different from what I see.'

I knew every inch of those five hundred yards, over which I had hopped and skipped and cycled, but to walk with Henryk felt new.

'You've left your front door open.'

'No one's going to steal anything from *my* house.'

We stood on a mound of earth that was piled up near the Watchtower tree. Perhaps it was another soil test made by the builders who planned still more new houses.

'I'll go first, shall I? So, what do I see? I see two rows of quite nice houses in new pink brick, either side of a wide white concrete highway, with tarmacadamed pavements and a red pillar box. The white road is straight and level, except towards the building site where no one yet lives. At the foot of the hill, as you approach Esper Road from Brightsea, there are older properties, from before the war and before the turn of the century. They are my other neighbours. They are not very friendly over the back fence. They don't think Esper Road should be here. They think our houses are ugly, and we are noisy, careless people who don't know how to live.'

'You can't see that, Henryk. You just know it.'

'Well observed, my dear! I certainly feel it. I only console myself with the near certainty that they won't invade and drive me out.'

I was jumping up and down. '*I* see two rows of box-like houses, like the houses in Monopoly, stretched out along the ridge of a long hill that used to be part of Esper House and the farm beside it. Sometimes I think they're just the knobbles on the backbone of some giant creature who is patiently keeping quite silent and still but might change his mind and rear up if we don't behave well. On other days I see them as a train of wagons, halted behind a leader on a mustang. Do you watch *Wagon Train*, Henryk? Well, you must know what a mustang is anyway, a sort of horse that prances and snorts in a halo of dust. We live in "The Settlement". We've just finished a long trek but we've been tough and we've kept faith and finally we've arrived here. I have a picture of reined-in horses, wagon wheels ceasing to turn, and happy women and children jumping down.'

Henryk put his hand on my shoulder. 'That's a much better picture than mine, Linka. I envy you. Only, everyone is good and busy in your world. Where have all the bad people gone?'

'Come on, I'll show you something I bet you haven't seen.'

I took him down the hill to the main road, where, as he said, the buildings were older, with high stone walls covered in ivy and moss, and the road was narrow. The buses had to hoot to let traffic know they were coming. We stopped at the pillar box.

'You see, VR, it stands for Queen Victoria in Latin, Victoria Regina, just like in our road it's Elizabeth Regina. In Victorian times children still died of tuberculosis and polio and going to the dentist really hurt! But it's sixty years since Queen Victoria died.'

'And almost as long since I was born. You look astonished! I'm exaggerating. I was born in nineteen fifteen. But it was another age. You're right, many things have got better. Come on. It's time for tea.'

'Is that why you listen to Beethoven so much, Henryk, because you don't believe things have got better? You must miss your family.'

'I miss many things.'

'Why aren't you a doctor any more?'

'Why am I not a doctor any more? Well, I'm a bit like you, I like to have time to watch what's happening in the world, and you know if you have a very busy and difficult job you can't do that. So I decided to choose an easy one. And then, when you are an observer of life you miss things less, because everything belongs to you.'

On Sunday morning I was brushing my teeth in the bathroom when I could see out of the window the ambulance in Henryk's drive. I dashed out. Hardly any cars came and went along Esper Road, except when a few dads left and returned from work during the week.

'Oh, swell, Henryk, can I see inside?'

He looked old that morning, like my grandfather in photographs. 'I'm on my way back, Linka. I'm not supposed to have the ambulance here. But you asked me if you could see it. Quick now.'

The high step up reminded me of climbing over a wrecked boat on the sea shore. Inside was dark blue and wood, with lots of shiny things, and cylinders for oxygen and two beds, either side of a little corridor like in a caravan. There were dials like clocks and a mask like the dentist used to give people gas before he pulled their teeth out, and a big white box with a red cross on it. Everything fitted together, like inside a wireless.

'Where do you sit? Show me.'

'Sometimes I drive, sometimes I sit with the patients, like this.'

'Do they cry?'

'No. It's usually... No, they don't cry. We give them medicine to make them sleepy.'

'Tranquillizers? My mum takes tranquillizers.' He shook his head. 'Henryk don't you sometimes miss being a doctor?'

'What I was saying the other day. That was another life. I have more time to watch what's going on like this.' He patted me on the knee. 'Now you'd better get out of this ambulance or people will say I'm trying to steal a little girl. I'll see you soon.'

Steal me? The school gardener Ian would steal me, but not Henryk.

We smacked our right palms together. '*Czeŝć!*' It sounded like it too. Cheshch.

'*Czeŝć! Dzien dobry, Henryk Braunschweig. Ich heisse* Linka

Beecham and I'm going to say a poem for you. *Wędrowiec, na istnienie spojrzawszy z ukosa / Wszedł na cmentarz: śmierć, trawa, niepamięć i rosa.'*

'Fantastic. *Doskonale!'*

On Saturday afternoon Dad's Labour Party friends came round and held a meeting in our kitchen, while I watched TV. It started earlier at weekends.

'Rubbish! Look, Mavis, Peter, unilateralism isn't a policy, it's suicide. The Russians will take Berlin and sit on our doorstep. The only way we can hope for peace is not to disarm ourselves but to rearm the Germans. The Germans are on our side now. Our enemy, alas that we have to have an enemy, but there it is, is Russia.'

'Soviet Russia is the only country in the world that has actually put socialism into practice. How can you call yourself Labour and not support them, Charles? What do you want the Labour party to be?'

'What do I want the Labour Party to be? An organization I can belong to with pride. But one which can change with the times. I joined when I was sixteen to further the rights of the working man. My father was out of work. My mother had to bring up four of us on less than nothing. But since then I've met other kinds of people, different types of socialist, and the world has moved on. We have democracy, we have the Welfare State and the Germans are consumed with remorse and need our help and approval to move on.'

I could see the difference between Dad and Peter Cannis. 'Dr' Cannis, as Bob Birkett called him, was thin, energetic and wore a jacket and tie. It was a red, knitted, fashionable tie with a square end, and he drove a car my mother loved, a Triumph Herald. I had the impression no one liked him, only as Mum said, 'he cut a dash'. No one else dressed so well.

'We cannot be socialists and pursue armed conflict. The Russians will give up nuclear weapons if we will.'

'I can imagine what kind of deal that would be, Peter. I worked alongside the Russians in Berlin.'

Dad was always reminiscing about how he was sent to Berlin just after the war ended, 'to help clear things up', 'to get things going again' and came away with a negative view of the Russians. He saw the gloom in their part of the city. He saw them being greedy at dinners. He saw them tearing up the railway lines to send back to Russia.

'Just because they had bad manners, Beech.'

'No, Mavis, because they weren't interested in cooperation. Because they were ready to set up a police state! Because all decisions were referred to Stalin. We used to feel sorry for their CO, who was afraid to speak in public. We went to their concerts to show willing and invited them back to our Shakespeare productions but they never came.'

'Disarmament will depend on weapons inspections on both sides. Humanity has no choice.'

Dad said Peter evidently had a hotline to humanity. 'Come off it, Peter, your peace is only another tactic. You're manipulating people's decent feelings. No one's against peace as such. You'd do anything to get Russian-style Communism here.'

'Is Soviet Communism so bad, Beech?' The voice was Bob Birkett's.

'It's coercive. It's close to Nazism.'

'How can you know? You've never been there.'

'Name me a so-called Communist in this country who has. Our socialism is a British kind. It is about equality and social justice for working people. It's nothing to do with Karl Marx.'

'It'll happen anyway, you see. It's the logic of history,' insisted Peter.

That made Dad shout. 'Your history, it's a new superstition and an old god. It means nothing except danger to the world.'

Our kitchen wasn't big enough for all the quarrels that took place when the Labour Party of Brightsea West came round. Mavis reminded them they were looking for a compromise on foreign policy issues, so they could put forward a coherent policy. Surely the main thing was 'to get the Tories out'. Of course, of course.

Dad sided with Mr Gaitskell as the Party leader to do the job.

'You haven't forgotten the debacle of 1959, by any chance?' The others wanted to see Mr Wilson replace him.

'They're all just politicians.' Leonard, a battered-looking older man whose surname I never knew, left the kitchen and lit a cigarette. One of Frieda's pictures hung on our wall, at 'the dining room end of the sitting room', and, whether he was short-sighted or drunk, or what, he talked to it. 'You can't trust politicians, that's what I say. You're fools if you believe they mean what they say. The truth – if it lies anywhere – lies in art. Isn't that so, dearie?' He addressed 'The Electric Woman', named by the painting and took another puff. 'Go on, light up for me, dearie. Have pity on an old man.' Leonard's voice sounded like wet gravel sliding down a shute.

I could hear Mavis starting afresh. She was Dad's favourite

colleague and so I liked her too. 'Beech, you want new houses and hospitals, and schools, and peace, but you would commit the Party to bombs, which would leave no cash for good things.'

'I can't deny it, Mavis. It's a contradiction we have to live with. We have bombs that say obey this rule or else! We don't expect to *use* them as bombs. But as rules they're very expensive, it's true.'

Peter Cannis insisted. 'What about Hiroshima? What about Nagasaki? Those bombs have already been used. And not by the Russians. By the Americans! Tens of thousands incinerated. And you want to go along with that? May your soul rot in hell!'

'It's what I believe is right.'

'And you think people will vote for that?'

'The people of this country want a new and fairer way of life. But they also have a sense of international responsibility.'

'We've lost an Empire, ho ho. Tell me something new.'

'Peter, the Empire made us feel responsible for the order and well-being of great swathes of the globe. You don't like to hear it because it's a different legacy of "international awareness" from the one you're trying to foist on us. But you can't make it go away. And it's why there will always be two approaches to disarmament in this country and two approaches to socialism. One inspired by Karl Marx, and by the Russian example, and one homemade, caught up in a world of British pride and prosperity and now boosted by all the patriotism – the self-congratulation, I admit – left over from the war.

'Internationally we want peace, of course. No decent human being could be against it, could they? And yet because of the Russians, who have their own idea of a world order, which we distrust, we have to hedge the issue of disarmament with all sorts of conditions. It would be irresponsible for us in the Labour Party to do anything else. Peace isn't a simple thing you either have or don't have, it's a compromise. It's like a leaking ship. The leaks have to be plugged to keep the vessel afloat. It takes hard work, plugging gaps, stopping breaches, hoping for the best, everyone pulling together, knowing there's disaster looming otherwise. The leaking ship theory is not logical, but it's realistic.

'There has to be some connection between *this* international outlook and what we want to do at home, namely make things fairer. I personally would make the electorate conscious of their British strengths and weaknesses, though I wouldn't pander to their jingoism like Churchill. Churchill belongs to a world that has gone for ever. I would paint a picture of the British legacy so people could see that the right post-war policy is social justice at home, combined with supporting a new world role for Germany, in the name of peace and prosperity. That's what the Labour Party must offer the post-war world.'

'While all the time actually preparing for war!' Peter Cannis shouted and invoked hellfire and rotting bodies over and over again. Finally he said Dad was betraying his origins, and that was somehow the nastiest thing he said and everyone went quiet.

Perhaps it was a silence of exhaustion. They just couldn't sort it out. *Wagon Train* had finished a while ago and I was standing between our sitting room and the kitchen listening to them.

'On the other hand,' began Mavis again, 'I'm afraid that Beech was right when he said we would have to fudge it.'

'I said nothing like that, Mavis!'

'But it's what you mean, Beech. Either we fudge it or we have

no power at all. You should know better, Peter. This country
may be anti-German and anti-European, Peter. But that doesn't
make it pro-Communist and unilateralist. That's your illusion,
down in Brightsea College.'

Leonard insisted, 'I *really* like this picture of "The Electric
Woman". Very after Picasso. Who's the artist, Chas?'

'My wife's sister.'

'That's the thing about art. It can reconcile differences that
just won't come together in life.'

'Very profound,' commented Peter Cannis, 'and utterly
bourgeois. I ask myself whether the new age will ever begin,
whether the essential *selfishness* of bourgeois life will ever be
overcome.'

Leonard liked Frieda. I liked Frieda. I liked the idea that we
had her paintings in our house. No one else had paintings like
that. Not the Robertsons, not Robbie's parents, not the
Birketts, not even Mrs Hill. I remembered the last time I saw
Frieda. We had tea in her house in South London, which was
full of pictures. Along every side of the room they were lined
up, leaning in towards the wall and the whole house smelled of
her paints, like the art room at school.

'Here, Linka, I found these photographs of your mother and
me wearing gas masks. That was taken outside our house,
before I went into the Wrens and Emma was evacuated. Gas
masks were horrible! What did they smell of? Cod-liver oil! And
the rubber was cold and stuck to your skin.'

'You look like Tank Monsters!'

'Go on, Linka, tell me what a Tank Monster is.'

'Monsters made of metal and lightbulbs, Frieda. They're on

television. They look like tanks from the war, but they have half-human faces and bodies. And they can exist at any time really. They could be in the future, or now, or in the past. Everyone's talking about them. They're a bit like "The Electric Woman". I think they were invented because of the war, when people got killed and had to kill people. They're something the inventor remembers as horrible: masks and armour and people hiding inside machines and killing each other.'

Though I could never imagine what Mum might find to do at Frieda's, where there was no television and it was cold and uncomfortable, she came back in a wild mood. She moved the table out of our living room, and tucked the turquoise chair under it, and pushed the settee against the wall, so she could dance. Dad said heaven knew how she dragged that great big table into the hall and what were we going to eat off. But she said family meals were a thing of the past and modern people needed light and space to be themselves. The wireless sat on the dining-room-end window sill and now she could jive with the volume button with nothing in her way. She turned the electrical contact off and on so the music, already with a strong elemental pulse, was delivered in sharp snatches.

'You'll break the set, Emma, I told you before.'

'You fool, you boring, stupid fool!'

Mrs Girton would soon be putting her kitchen steps up to the back fence. Soon they would really be talking in Esper Road!

'He's from Poland.'

'But he has a German name, I heard him tell Charles Beecham.'

'Emma Beecham!'

'She's always dissatisfied.'

'She needs to get a grip, that woman, at her age!'

'She's thirty-three, the same age as me.'

'Charles needs our sympathy, with a wife like that.'

'And that surly child, out at all hours...'

Then it felt as though there was a kind of truce. Mum was cooking.

She took a steaming pyrex from the oven and set it down on the dining room table, now returned to its old situation between the kitchen and the window on to the garden.

'Didn't Granny have a gong for mealtimes?' Something good about the days before life was modern popped into my head.

'The house was enormous.'

'That must have been nice. Lots of hiding places. Lots of room for adventures, like in books.'

'It had character,' Mum replied mysteriously.

The recipe she used was still in the kitchen, torn from a magazine. She had poured a tin of condensed mushroom soup over some pork chops and baked them together. She opened a tin of peas. The potatoes were from a packet. Just add water and a swirl of butter to make instant mashed potato with no washing-up. Stir with a wooden spoon to avoid lumps. Serve immediately, or dot with more butter and brown under the grill. We ate greedily, like Russians, I suspected. Maybe that was the reason Dad didn't want to pick up his chop bone, not to be like a Russian in Berlin, but Mum said he was prissy.

'Anyone seen my milk bottle tops?' I asked when we'd

finished and they were drinking tea. Neighbours had begun leaving them on our doorstep.

Mum produced them. 'Take them away soon. They smell.'

'I'm collecting for the RSPCA to stop cruelty to dogs. The cruellest thing is the Russians sending dogs into space.'

'I don't suppose the RSPCA can do anything about that,' said Dad.

'What do the Russians want with a few smelly old bits of silver paper? You are a funny girl, Lynne-Caroline.'

'No, Mummy, you don't understand, the milk tops get sold for scrap metal and then with the *money* we pay the Russians to let the dogs have a happy life in retirement. On earth. When they come back. They say they don't know *how* to bring the dogs back, but they must find a way soon, mustn't they? So we have to raise money to help their research. Although I don't know why they have to bother sending dogs up there at all.'

My father put his teacup down. 'I understand you don't want the dogs hurt, Linka. But don't you believe in space exploration? It means progress. For progress there have to be some sacrifices.'

'You mean like God calling on Abraham to kill his son Isaac on a bonfire, Dad? But God changed his mind and made a sheep appear, which was all right because sheep were *meant* for cooking.' My heathen dad looked bewildered. 'I mean I just don't understand why the people who want to find out about the moon don't go up themselves.'

Eventually Dad said, 'It's nothing to do with God, Linka. Haven't we talked about these things before? There's no such thing as God.'

He kept saying this about God and I couldn't accept it.

My mum intervened. 'We could do with getting things right on earth first. That's what I think.'

Right, Mum, right! They seemed almost happy that weekend. But when Dad asked me after school what I talked to Mr Braunschweig about Mum burst into tears. Brown Shw-eye-g, he said. Good for Dad.

Mum disappeared upstairs. I could hear her sobbing and the bed springs bouncing. I showed Dad the stamps Henryk had given me. 'Much nicer than ours.' The big triangular stamps featured targets of Socialist production, the glory of the armed forces, and Dzerzhinsky, founder of the Soviet secret police.'

'So our Polish friend is a Communist?'

'He's not on any side. His wife's a Communist though. That's why he left. No, he hates Poland being a Communist country. He told me it was even like Germany under Hitler. They have Polish Gestapo, you know, Dad. They're the secret police. Not the good police.'

'But why should you be so interested, Linka? You're only a child.'

Dad was out at another of his meetings when the door bell rang. I thought it was the popman but when I opened the door it was Henryk, holding an LP record. He had brushed his hair back from his face and looked very clean, though older. He was a bit suntanned, which went nicely with the blue shirt. 'Hello, Linka, how are you? Is your mother in?'

'Mum!' I shrieked. The polite way was to go and fetch her, but I didn't dare move from the spot.

She came from the kitchen and switched the TV off on her way. She always did that when visitors came.

'Lynne-Caroline, put the kettle on, dear.' That 'dear' was a bad sign. She didn't normally call me that.

Henryk hesitated then sat on the settee. The atmosphere was rather tense between them, but friendly. As I waited for the kettle to whistle, and warmed the pot, 'settee' reminded me of 'teepee', a word from Westerns.

'Have you ever slept in a tent, Henryk?'

'Linka, not now!' Mum ordered me to go upstairs and change.

When I came back my tea was cold. I took a biscuit I didn't want in order to catch up on what they were saying. He told her what I knew. He had left when he could. Of course it was difficult. His qualifications counted for nothing. But sometimes you have to decide to make a new life. Then my mother was off talking about Lincolnshire. He grew looser, but also more attentive, as she spoke, as that part of him which was a doctor responded to her. As for the part of him which was a man he never had any doubts. 'Look, I brought you this record, I thought you might like it.'

We only had a small record-player, a pick-up, which came in a grey and gold fleck design and smelled of plastic, and we kept it on the floor. When her flared skirt spread out as she slotted the record into place and slid the arm across it, she was like a gorgeous bird laying an egg. She stood up and then the voice of Frank Sinatra, like air pumped into a balloon, lifted the whole room off the ground. The voice was light and full of lyricism and joy. Her whole tiny face brightened, for she too loved music. I ran to join her to dance, clutching her round the middle and placing my feet beside hers. She pushed me away.

'Linka, go out to play. Will you go out to play?'

'But I want to hear what Henryk says about the war.'

'Mr Braunschweig—'

'No, he's not, he's Henryk. And he was my friend first.'

I avoided Henryk's eye, went to the back door, pulled on my boots, and hurled myself through the ash trees into the open field.

'Emma, I cannot write English well. I find that you are a lovely woman. I'm here when you need me. Or you can send the child with a note. She often comes to see me.'

'Dear Henryk, I never thought I would meet a man like you. Mostly I have bad luck. I feel there's a curse on me, and the child makes it worse. Otherwise I would leave Charles. I've never loved him. He's a fool. And not good enough for a Luck-Carter.'

'Should you blame the child? I talked to her today... and I don't think she will mind about us.'

'I do blame her. She's mad. I'm afraid of her. She won't stop talking about the war and collecting strange things.'

'Simple women used to believe that if there was something wrong with their child, or they didn't love it, then they'd given birth to a devil.'

'Then I'm simple! She reminds me of all the mad people I have known: my sister Dorothy... and the terrible woman I lived with during the war. I feel I'm going to choke, I can't breathe, there isn't enough space for all of us to live and I'm not mad so they've got to let me be free. Let me out.'

'Emma, take that space. Imagine it all around you. Take it in music and dancing and laughing. Only not in getting stuck in your own head.'

'Why do you love me? What's lovable about me? I'm messed up.'

'I love you because of that. One has to have seen suffering.'

'It's strange you like my daughter so. Charles doesn't like it.'

'I feel deep sympathy with the child. She and I experience everything with the passion of the half-excluded. You're jealous, Emma, that's crazy. Linka is a child.'

'Be a doctor again. Show them you're someone!'

'You want me to be someone important again so you can leave your husband and marry me. But Emma, that's not what I want. I want warmth where I can find it, without thinking too much. I want a little contact, to keep me going.'

'I cannot bear uncertainty.'

'And yet you must have change.'

'Dorothy was supposed to be my friend. But she was never normal, so they put her in a home. They took her away from me. Then the Pickles never accepted me. Oh, Henryk, they were so cruel.'

'So you want to do the same with Linka?'

'But I can't live with Lynne-Caroline.'

'You hate your husband too.'

'We Luck-Carters were smart. Look where he's brought me!'

'Linka told me her granny was a suffragette.'

'My mother left me alone. She never cared for me.'

'So you don't care for Linka. You're taking your revenge.'

'Life hurts me.'

'Do you believe in evil? I think you do. Only you think it was invented specially to harm you. That's wrong. It's out there as a threat to all of us. Some people believe that good wins over evil, and they know what good is, and they think that this battle was won after the end of the war. But all people and peoples do good and bad things. Good deeds were done by Germans in the

war, and some bad deeds were committed by Britain, as well as
the other way round. Only can we live with that knowledge?
Can we live with knowing that none of our motives is pure,
even when the outcome is good?'

'Let's die together.'

'You don't mean that. You're a child. You have everything to
live for.'

'What an era is ours for a child to grow up in, with the threat
of the Bomb!'

'That's an excuse. Those words mean nothing to you.'

'I wish there was something I wanted to do, to paint, to read,
to take an interest in *something*. I look at Frieda's paintings and
I wonder. But if I drew or modelled anything it would have no
lines to hold it in, no boundaries, I would turn my back and it
would fall apart, disappear, vanish. Nothing stays, nothing is
permanent. You lose everything. Being alive is feeling loss.'

'Say you love me, Emma.'

'There's a machine Lynne-Caroline likes to go on. It's a grab
which moves about in a see-through box of treasures. When you
put the money in the slot it looks as if it might scoop up a prize.
I paid a penny for Lynne-Caroline to see one of those grabs in
action outside the newsagent's. That toy never grabbed
anything, Henryk! Just as its jaws opened, and it grazed the top
of the treasure pile, the power switched off! You couldn't win.
I complained, of course.'

'You're right to complain.'

The school gardener had spotted a dead woodpecker at the far
end of the sports field. 'Behind the goal posts, under the trees,
ma'am.'

When no one was around he talked to me and offered me sweets. I never told anyone about that although I thought about it when I went to talk to Henryk. Ian had a thick neck with deep cracks in it, which was always reddish-brown from being outside in the sun. I never took his sweets, even though I wanted them, and I walked in a big circle to avoid him. Only today I had my task, dispensed by Miss Rogers, to miss registration in order to recover the body of the bird. I pulled a face at him and walked on.

At nine in the morning, glistening with dew, the school grounds spread out beyond the playground in a stillness which recalled to me the stillness of the building site on a summer evening. The woodpeckers must have lived there for many years before the school was built, in the grounds of some other grand house, razed to make way for us newcomers 'after the war'. The rest of the visible past was demolished, but the birds stayed as part of God's plan. They looked as if their feathers were made of the brightest and finest silk embroidery, and each time one died, and we buried it, it was a tribute to their beauty, Miss Rogers said. We should notice such things.

Miss Rogers, who wasn't married, whose life was the school, stood at her window watching me, as I walked across the field carrying a grey cushion. The field was soaked with the kiss of morning, but under the great green curtain of branches at the far end, the brown loam was dry and powdery. The crêpe-rubber soles of my sandals squeaked on the grass like hers on the linoleum, then fell silent in that goblin land. Crouching, I raised the cold woodpecker in cupped hands and set it on the cushion. I remembered when I had caught the stoat in the pit and became amazed at all the things my human hands could do: write, stroke, hit, point, capture, release. With the dead bird on its bier I processed back towards the school.

Miss Rogers was fit. She sometimes joined us in the gym class and showed us that she could still touch her toes. She sprang from her door and came round outside as I appeared. 'Wait there, Linka!' Back inside she asked a passing child to fetch Robbie and Bettina and Alan. I waited beside the playground. When they arrived, pretending they hadn't been running before they came into her sight, she began.

'What a magnificent specimen we have to inter today!' On formal occasions Miss Rogers spoke in her official voice, using unusual words.

We walked towards the near end of the sports ground and took the path beside the deserted playground towards the high rhododendron hedges, which marked one of our boundaries. Everyone else was working now and we gulped back our sense of privilege. I remembered some of her words from assembly.

'We are here to celebrate what human beings, in the family, in the nation, and even alone, can do, and what must continue, what shall continue, from age to age. World without end. Amen.'

The monster who sits patiently with the houses of Esper Road on his back does not yet want this world to end. The Monster and God are of one accord.

She smoothed the apple-green silky breast of the bird with one finger.

'Where shall I dig, Miss Rogers?' Robbie had forgotten his pullover and shivered.

'Take about ten paces in from the path, Robbie.'

He dug in a patch at the foot of the bushes. The strain showed in his bony face. He had to stand on the fork with two

feet at once and sway about like a drunk on stilts to achieve any
depth.

Alan said, 'You'll never manage to dig a foot deep like that.'

'Now boys!' But Robbie by now was on his knees, scooping
out the last loose earth with his hands. Then Alan lowered the
dye-bright carcass into the hole, and covered it with earth.
Finally Miss Rogers dropped her hand and Bettina in a small
high voice, with scant regard for meaning or punctuation, read:

> And he shewed me a pure river of water of life, clear as
> crystal, proceeding out of the throne of God and of the
> Lamb.
>
> In the midst of the street of it, and on either side of the
> river, was there the tree of life, which bare twelve manner of
> fruits, and yielded her fruit every month: and the leaves of
> the tree were for the healing of the nations.
>
> And there shall be no more curse: but the throne of God
> and of the Lamb shall be in it; and his servants shall serve
> him:
>
> And they shall see his face; and his name shall be in their
> foreheads.
>
> And there shall be no night there; and they need no
> candle, neither light of the sun; for the Lord God giveth
> them light; and they shall reign for ever and ever.
>
> Amen.

Bettina lowered the heavy book with a noisy show of relief. Alan
and Robbie continued to push and shove each other in a way
meant to be imperceptible to Miss Rogers. She noticed but stood
with her fair grey head bowed, hands linked in the lap of the

tailored and vented linen skirt which ended two inches below
her knee. She reminded me of Ceri, my granny, she of the tough
breed. But suddenly, staring down at the earth covering the bird,
I doubted absolutely that the Lord God giveth light. This place
would always be night and bones. Later, in our art lesson, I tried
to paint the woodpecker, but I couldn't even remember what it
looked like. The green and red splodge on the paper was a mess.
I threw the water jar on the floor and burst into tears.

From today Linka Beecham will sit on her own. That had been
a bad day. It was now six months since I had a desk to myself
to mark my distinction from the other children. I was top of the
class by a wide margin. The idea of Arlingham school was that
I should remain that way. So I sat every day in a place where no
one's elbow jogged me and no one distracted me from my
purpose.

'Eh, eh, teacher's pet! You really like her, don't you? Stupid.
She's just a silly cow. No one will marry her. No one will marry
you if you're not careful.'

We had taken our exam, the purpose of our existence that
year, and now the papers had been marked and we knew our
new schools. I was going in September to Brightsea Girls'
Grammar. I had passed the 11+. Bettina was going to the
secondary modern. She had not.

'To be what?' I asked, to have an excuse to draw close to her
blonde hair and blue eyes and white skin. She was perfect like a
doll.

'Do I have to be something, Linka?' Out of the pert little
mouth tumbled a cascade of silver laughter.

'Yes, you must. My father says—'

'You be something then! I'm going to get married to a nice boy. You can't do that. You've got boy's hair.'

Just after we had the exam results I was walking to the bus stop alone when Bettina and Danny and a fat girl from the bottom of the class whom I had never spoken to sprang out and pulled me into a red phone box. Danny, who was 'going with' Bettina, held my arms.

'Now, Linka, we're going to turn you into a girl. Just keep still and it won't hurt.' Giggling, Bettina, who had set her bag of tricks on the shelf above Button A, stippled my face with powder. I jerked my head back so my hair was in Danny's face, and tried to bang his nose, but he had my arms in a vice. Bettina dotted rouge on my cheeks. She spat on her cake of mascara and got the fat girl to reach in and force my chin up. I bit the fat girl, but the mascara brush went in my eye. I bit the lipstick too, and it stuck in my teeth and my mouth.

'And just to finish,' cried Bettina, and she sprayed me all over with sticky hair spray from Woolworths which made my eye even redder.

Danny changed to a single arm lock while he ruched up my dress and tugged on my bra strap. (The garment from Jennings had taken possession of my body.) Danny pushed me backwards and forwards on the elastic like one of those jocari balls you hit and it comes back to you.

The fat girl pulled my knickers down and yelled, 'Look, she is a girl. She has got one,' and she was like a spider crawling on my legs. I kicked out but she held my foot.

'Hold her again, Danny.'

'Now, Linka Beecham, don't you look pretty? Hahahahahaha.' Bettina held up a pink dressing-table mirror

on a handle so I could see. She must have brought it specially
from home.

Afterwards my eyes stung so much it looked as if I was
crying, and I walked the three miles home, so that not even the
bus conductor, a familiar figure, in a uniform, should see me.

Miss Rogers invited me to her room. I had written a story about
how I got lost on holiday in Lincolnshire because my mother
got bored and left for somewhere more interesting, but then I
met a German soldier, to whom I said '*Ich heisse Linka*', and
everything was all right. Because we spoke the same language,
he could show me the way home. I wrote another story about
God feeling lonely, sitting high up in a tower, where no one
came to say hello.

I peered into her pale face, behind the gold-rimmed
spectacles. It was a cross face, girls like Bettina said, because
Miss Rogers had no husband, but I saw love for me.

'Sit down, my dear! My chairs don't bite, you know. That's
better.' It was so silent in Miss Rogers's room I thought the
world had stopped like on the building site at night. No one
dared make a sound passing in the corridor. But the silence also
grew out of her extreme concentration on me.

'Is there a book you'd like to borrow?' she asked after a
while. 'I've some lovely new ones. Have a look. Take your time.
I've my reports to be going on with.' I chose a white-covered
book of Old Testament stories, and sat cross-legged on the
floor, lifting the tissue paper and ogling the pictures beneath.
They were coloured in blue and mauve and gold and ivory, like
stained glass windows flooded with sunlight. They hurt me
with their beauty. If you press against a loose tooth, that hurts

too, and you enjoy the pain, because the tooth wants to come out. The pain and pleasure mount and whoosh, suddenly a new peace descends. But I didn't know what to do about so much beauty in the pictures in a book, so I looked for scenes I recognized. David slaying Goliath, Abraham asked to sacrifice Isaac, but slaughtering a sheep instead. There was the flood and the rainbow. And Moses leading the Israelites. For more than half an hour the almost square room overlooking the staff garden at Arlingham, in a prize-winning design for 1955 by Adrian Bell, was filled with silence. Miss Rogers and I were so happy in that room that she invited me to drop in every Wednesday afternoon, instead of class silent reading.

'Do you think it's because of her upbringing?'

Mr Fleming, who was also there on Wednesdays, had the softest face and the quietest voice I had ever seen and heard in a man. I had the impression he was pretending not to be there, and that made me quieter still.

'I don't, Miss Rogers. This kind of thing is in the genes. They sometimes grow out of it. Only the child gets so sensitive and so passionately wrapped up in her world she can do herself damage. The religious enthusiasm particularly.'

'Describe yourself, Linka.'

Well, I didn't think I was a boy. I just wasn't wholly a girl, or probably something else again. Once my mother said she thought I was like her sister Frieda. Frieda is a painter. Another time like her mad sister Dorothy.

'That's interesting. Your auntie is a painter.'

I pictured Frieda that last time I had seen her in London, with her tall, athletic figure and her ageing face and hair,

compared with my mother. Frieda painted 'belatedly in the
Cubist style', I heard the adults say. She used a lot of greys and
mauves, and with some heavy black outlines in the canvas we
didn't hang (it lived in the spare room and was called 'People
in a Waiting Room'), and browns and yellows and earth tones
in that one we did, the one Leonard liked, 'The Electric
Woman'.

'It's a picture of a woman made of wire and lightbulbs and
with bosoms like light switches.'

Mr Fleming laughed too heartily. 'That's good. Bosoms like
light switches.'

Miss Rogers took him aside. 'I had her mother up here once
asking if "Lynne-Caroline" couldn't be sent to a special school.
She wanted her sent to Alexander Neill!'

'The Summerhill dream,' replied Mr Fleming. 'The idea of a
school, and a life, in which people do exactly as they wish when
they wish it because that is what their being needs at that
moment. It was what Neill wished for himself, after his stern
upbringing. It would be a place where no one need obey a rule.'

'I can't think of a worse place for Linka. She would be lost
there. She would go under.'

'But no doubt Mrs Beecham would like it. She would like to
live her childhood again. Whichever we have, rules or freedom,
we always believe that the opposite leads to happiness.'

'Maybe I can help you, Emma. I'd like to help. It's all that's left
to me in life.' Henryk patted the seat beside him on the settee.
'Let's listen to some music. Come and sit beside me.' He played
my mother that exquisitely tender violin concerto by Beethoven
which he had been playing the first afternoon I visited him,

when the rat was killed. He held her like a baby while they listened.

'What you need is a big space around you, Emma. Some people do. We all vary in the amount of space we need to *imagine* around us. Think it in your imagination, Emma, and fill it with your inventions and don't worry what anyone thinks. Just live in your space alongside them. Find that space in music.'

They were peaceful and sad and Mum had bare feet. 'A big space, Henryk? I'll try.' She sounded tearful.

'Keep thinking you have a big space around you in which you can stretch out... and listen to music.'

It was five o'clock. I thought he ought to go. Finally he slipped the record into its cardboard sleeve and held it like his doctor's bag.

'I'm ahead of my time, Henryk,' said Emma. 'People will see. I'm an individual.'

'Because you lost Dorothy, and your mother wasn't there, you found it hard to love anyone. You were too afraid for yourself. In my case, loss was just... numbing... or rather, what I felt was that the world was no longer to do with me. I had feelings, but I felt them at a distance, as if someone had given me a little notebook and told me to write down my observations on mankind. As a way of living. I have taken a step back from fully living. Or at least I had, until I met you.'

'Was your wife pretty?'

'I'm sure she still is. She's remarried – a man with views similar to her own. They believe in the State they live in, that they are doing something good.'

'Was she beautiful?'

'*I* thought so.'

'But not more beautiful than me.'

'Emma, you're a child.'

She got up and danced for him, to some sort of wild music that had a lot of stamping in it, though it began quietly. Her arms she held up straight, against her ears, with the fingers knotted; as her head tilted, the arms moved from the vertical like a great clock hand. Henryk sat forward in the chair with pursed lips, half-smiling, half-grimacing. He was a man who had moved across Esper Road into timelessness. When she stepped out of her dress and unhooked her brassiere her skin was brown, with white bikini marks.

He said, 'Show me what it feels like to be alive.'

They both ended up crying.

'This violent world we live in, Emma, so fierce, so cruel, and we are asked to dance to it. Come to me.'

I got up a petition to save the Russian dogs. My mother spoke darkly of 'those nasty Russians' and said, 'I'll sign your petition, Lynne-Caroline.' She wrote in a hand that sloped backwards, something Arlingham didn't allow.

I combined enlisting people to sign the petition with my usual Saturday quest for milk bottle tops. 'Hello, it's Linka Beecham from number seventeen. I'm sorry to bother you but I was wondering whether you had any milk bottle tops for the RSPCA. The situation has become especially urgent because we have to raise money to save the Russian dogs in space.'

At number five I didn't knock because Diana Emsworth had put her gold tops out on the back step. I would have liked to go in and pat Macnamara but Mum recently told Dad that

Stephen Emsworth specialized in divorces – 'When the time comes I'll know where to go' – so I didn't feel I could put a foot in the Emsworth house.

At number thirteen Susan Birkett said she was sorry, but her kids had decided to collect their own tops. That made me terribly cross. 'I bet Rosalie and Jono haven't thought of a good cause.'

'We can't all be as clever as you, Linka.'

I forgot to ask her to sign.

Mrs Girton only took two pints of stripy-topped homogenized a week, so it was hardly worth knocking. Besides she might ask me about Mum's dancing again and the open windows and I couldn't tell her the made-up story of the bird again.

The Hills were a better bet. There was always something going on at number twenty-three. They had lots of card and board games and jigsaws and they made up quizzes, and on Saturday mornings their mum taught them French.

'Hello, it's Linka Bee—' And they sat me down and I had orange and said *bonjour* and *merci* and Mrs Hill signed.

'How are you, Linka?' Mrs Hill peered at me. '*Comment vas-tu?* And how is your mother, and your poor father?'

'Linka, I've been looking for you. Where have you been?' It was Robbie on his bicycle. 'Here, from my mum. Can I come with you to do the rest? Dr Pandraneth said he's waiting for us before he goes out.' At number twenty-five, immediately next to the new houses still being built, lived Dr Pandraneth from India. He was a nice man and he used to make us laugh with the funny words he used.

'The *airly* bird catches the worm, but not today, Linka?'

Robbie giggled. 'Do you mean she's late, sir?'

'Well, young man, she's certainly not airly.'

When I told him about the Russian dogs, Dr Pandraneth said he admired the British Empire but he wasn't going to sign anything. I couldn't make sense of that. Robbie was of the opinion that they always talked in proverbs in India so we recited all we knew to each other in case we ever went there.

'Early to bed, early to rise, makes a man healthy, wealthy and wise.'

'A bird in the hand is worth two in the bush.'

'Waste not want not.'

Dr Pandraneth's wife appeared. She wore a sari and wasn't much bigger than me. It should have been embarrassing. We were imitating them. But she laughed. 'Linka, does a vooman vant to be vise? I think she'd rather stay in bed, no?'

Was she talking about my mum? I didn't know. I took the tops home and fetched my bike.

Sen apeared and ran along behind, holding on to my saddle.

'Heh, Sen, you have to sign my petition. You like dogs, don't you? Or are they pesky things?'

He wore narrow Teddy boy trousers and wasn't working that day. I often wondered how old he was, eighteen or nineteen perhaps. He said, 'Which way you goin', Linka? I could do with a lift.'

'Sign first!' I fished the lined paper out of my saddlebag.

''and it over then. I can't sign nothin' unless you' and it over. an' a pen.'

'I've given you the pen.'

'So you 'ave. There you are, Linka. Now I really mus' be goin'.'

I counted my list of names. 'Look, he's drawn a fox.'

'That's because he can't write,' said Robbie.

At number twenty-two Mike was fixing his car. We could see his feet sticking out. Robbie peered under the chassis from the other side.

'What's that?' Mike wriggled clear, his face streaked with oil.

'I didn't say anything,' smiled Robbie.

'Not to worry, son. While you're there, do us a favour and pass us that spray can.'

Sheena opened the yellow front door and groaned. 'That husband of mine loves that car more than he does me, I swear. Do you want to come in for a bit, kids?' We looked at each other, but we weren't going to say no. Sheena's house was airless and smelled of nappies. But it also smelled of bacon, and we left with lots of tops, and the sweetness from two chocolate digestive biscuits clinging to our teeth.

'Russians, Linka, they're not very nice, are they? That Stalin sticking people in camps. But isn't he dead now?'

'I'm not sure. I'll have to ask my dad.'

'I'll sign anyway and for Mike.' We went out on the doorstep. She shouted, 'I'll sign for you, Mike, OK, that you don't like the way the Russians are sending animals into space?'

'You do that, love. Bloody Reds.'

'How many signatures have you got now?'

'Twelve.'

As we came away from Sheena and Mike's, Robbie was thoughtful. 'My mum says we should say "auntie" and "uncle" to older people. To be polite.'

I demurred. I called them Sheena and Mike.

'Your family's so modern, Linka.'

I decided not to hear. 'Anyone left?'

'Just Henryk and Mr Woolacott, but Mr Woolacott never gives anything.'

'The Polish man? You go alone then, Linka. Mum says I'm not supposed to play with you because of what your mum's getting up to. She'll save tops for you, but you're a bad girl to play with.'

'A hammer, Linka?'

'I want to build things, Dad. Please, I won't lose it, and if I do I'll buy you a new one out of my pocket money.'

I built the next den alone in another oak tree which must have been a hundred years old. I was so sure the tree was Victorian, and used to stand in the garden of Esper House, on the edge of the pony field where the happy children played, that I decided to live there. The trunk rose sheer for the first eight feet, then opened out in a calyx of thick branches. If I stood on the fence post and hung on to that twiggy bit, I reckoned I could get a foothold in the hollow and swing my leg over the big branch. I tried. But the twig was in the wrong place and I had nothing to pull myself up by. So I had to fetch Dad's tow rope. But I didn't ask for it. I couldn't keep begging for things and besides, Dad wasn't there until late and I didn't like going back when he was out.

I climbed up and pulled up the rope behind me. I straddled the broad oak beam, dangling my legs. I had the tape measure from Woolworths and calculated what I needed. Late, very late, when it was half dark, I took planks and nails from the building site.

Work was slow, because I could only raid in the evening and I was alone. In my impatience I chose any wood which was the right length, so beside the unshakeable planks lay flimsier pieces unsuited to the purpose I gave them. At the same time the project grew. I wanted not just a floor, but walls and a roof. I took a massive shortcut by wedging a piece of plasterboard in place.

'Hello, Mrs March, this is Linka Beecham. From Arlingham. Can I speak to Bettina, please?'

'Bettina, this is Linka from school.'

'Hahahahahaha.'

I laughed too, though the palms of my hands prickled. 'I've built this amazing den. I thought you and Danny would like to come and see. And Patrick and Michael.'

Bettina came in her tight-waisted and full-skirted party dress, with silver shoes. She tossed her blonde head, made with her little foot to step into some non-existent stirrup but quickly gave up. 'It's impossible. What do you want to climb up there for anyway?' Michael volunteered to let her stand on his back. But she didn't like that so we all gave up and sat on the grass.

Patrick said, 'It's not a bad treehouse. But what are you going to do with it?'

'Look out on things. Maybe sleep there, even live there eventually.'

Bettina giggled and turned to Danny. 'See if you can drink out of this cup at the same time as me.' She put the cup of pop on the grass and they shimmied up to it on their stomachs like two serpents about to touch tongues.

My working position was now about fourteen feet off the ground, with the second floor under me, for I was engaged in composing the second-storey walls. When I hammered, the whole house shook.

'Hello, Linka.' The voice, a mixture of timidity and admiration, belonged to Anne Hill. Some lookout I was! I didn't notice anyone coming.

Anne was with her mother and Amy, like matching dolls in different sizes, all three staring up at me. Mrs Hill said what I had made was very ugly. Anne looked up expectantly. What would I reply to her mother? Something rude?

'Does your mother know what you're up to?'

'Oh yes,' I lied.

'Then she's an even more careless woman than I thought. I shall have to have a word. It's an eyesore, Linka. And the tree? It's a living thing. Don't you mind hurting it?'

'I'm sorry, Mrs Hill, but I have to build my den. And it has to be high up so I can see everything.'

She shook her head, called Anne away from the dangling tow rope, and walked back home with her hands on the shoulders of her two daughters.

Some time after that Robbie appeared, Robbie who had been ordered to stay away. 'Heh, Linka, the men are coming from the site! Quick! Quick! All that wood you've stolen.' He sounded close to tears. I threw down my hammer and jumped down from the ceiling where I was working. Next minute I was tumbling through the air, in a whirlwind of motley bits of wood. My long-rehearsed preparations for skydiving proved useless. I crashed through the treehouse floor and hit the ground with a tremendous thud, flat on my back.

'Linka!'

A sound escaped me like a horse coughing. 'Uuuuur! Uoooor!'

'Linka, don't die!' cried Robbie, jumping up and down.

'Good thing she din' 'it the fence.' The voice belonged to Sen. 'Eh, what's 'appened to you, big girl?' I couldn't speak. He picked me up in his arms. 'There now, you juss let Sen carry you 'ome.'

He carried me across his body all the way up the field behind our house, his hair exuding a smell of grease, and his breath ripe with cigarettes. But I was weak with shock and everything hurt, so I just lay there, spread out, and closed my eyes. Robbie walked behind like a wake following a coffin. I heard him say that the men had gone down to inspect the treehouse and it was good we'd got away.

Sen whispered in my ear, 'Nice little tits, eh? Gettin' real grown up these days.'

I was uncomfortable the way he was holding me. But I couldn't move.

'We'd better go in. My mum may be out.'

There was no one downstairs. But then we met Henryk on the stairs, in a shirt and trousers but bare feet, and my mother behind him in her dressing gown.

'She aint 'alf winded 'erself, Mrs Beecham, couldn't breathe for a while.'

'Oh, Lynne-Caroline, for goodness' sake, you do get up to some things. Put her in there, would you? Lay her down.'

'The air just wasn' pumpin' in and out of 'er chest. Still it's all right now.'

'I'll have a look at her,' said Henryk, coming forward to the bed, rolling back his sleeves and sitting down beside me. 'I'm a doctor.'

'I thought you was an ambulance man.'

'Both.'

My mother thanked the boys and sent them away, closed the curtains and pulled off my clothes. I didn't want to be naked in front of Henryk but everything hurt. When I lay down again, she bathed my cheeks and forehead with a warm flannel and I fell asleep.

'I've arranged to take all my holiday. I shall be away six weeks. Don't object, Emma. You are the child's mother. I'll not leave you short of money.'

I was in my room trying to write with a feather I had found in the garden.

'Tell Daddy his taxi's here.' She put her head round the door. She didn't know what to do. My father had a raincoat on even though it was a sunny day, and carried a leather suitcase with metal corners, and a canvas grip. As she lingered in the hall, he squeezed past her.

'You do those Germans some good now. No one else likes them.' She turned to me. 'Wave goodbye to Daddy then!'

'I *am* waving.'

Mavis had come round and told Dad he would never get the Labour Party nomination for the by-election while there was so much talk about my mum.

'It's hypocritical, but that's the way things are, alas. You're a good man, and we're wasting you. But I don't see a way out at the moment. Bob knows what they're saying in the town.'

They sat in deckchairs the garden, where I brought them tea.

He sat with his eyes closed, leaning forward, with his hands over his face. It seemed to me odd that when Dad was sad the birds were tweeting and there was a bright blue sky.

'I'm sorry, Beech. But look, it may be for the best.' They sat for a while. Dad had made a garden full of bright colours.

'I don't want to divorce her.'

'But you want a political career.'

'They're just using this thing with Emma.'

'When Peter said you'd betrayed your origins that was nonsense, but you know, Beech, you are a bit exotic for Brightsea. You've been places no one else has. You speak German.'

'And yet I'm still a nobody with no formal qualifications. That matters too. I'm caught. Who was it in literature who was taken to the top of a high mountain and shown all the riches of the world and told they could be his if only he fitted in?'

'Jesus.'

'Can't be.'

'The thing is, Beech, what are you going to do about Emma? I don't like to see you suffer.'

'The question for me is this: am I married to a sick woman or just to one who doesn't love me? When I know the answer I will know what to do.'

'Will a bit of distance help? On the Council we're building up this link with Heilsheim. You could go as Brightsea's representative this summer. After all, you speak German. And then you would have some time to decide. Think about it, Beech.'

'I can't bear to stay here.'

So I was about to lose Dad too, and now the whole summer holidays loomed, without school.

After Mavis's visit Dad and I went up to London to see Frieda. We had buck rarebits in the dining car of the train, and he drank lager and I had lemonade. Then we went back to our compartment, which we had to ourselves. Mum would have liked that. She liked space. Space to breathe, she said. Dad read a newspaper while I stared out at the passing fields. He sighed and said out loud that he didn't know which Party he could belong to in the end and maybe it was fate rescuing him from the narrow choices of British politics. He couldn't be a Conservative with his background, and however hard Gaitskell might try, Labour would never really care about Europe, so who could he even vote for, let alone represent.

'Don't be in a hurry to grow up, Linka. There's too much to sort out.'

'When I grow up I don't think I'll get married.' I thought of Miss Rogers. I could be like her. I could love the beauty of birds and prayers and wear flat, squeaky shoes.

'Oh, no, you must get married.'

Then we were chugging into the dirty, sooty big city. The sight of it changed his mood. 'Look, Linka, here's where I used to live as a boy. The one with the aerial on the roof.'

I stared at the back of a long row of terraced houses with H-shaped TV aerials along the railway line. 'There's a lot of aerials, Dad.'

'This one.' He pressed his finger impatiently against the window. The tall houses of yellow-grey brick were all dark with soot from the passing engines and it was impossible to tell one from another.

'Alan Robertson's only got a toilet outside.'

'They'll be moving in the autumn. Mavis told me the Council has some lovely new flats.'

'I don't think they want to move to a flat.'

'They won't know it till they get there.'

'But Dad, we wouldn't like it if someone came along and said you have to move out of your house. We wouldn't like that. I would sit down and refuse to go.'

'And you would be stubborn and silly.'

I chewed my lip.

In London we stood in the queue for the black taxis, which drove right into the huge station, almost on to the train platform. 'Don't go far, Linka.'

'I'll just explore quickly.' Steam rose from the newly-arrived engines, and there was the gorgeous smell of a coke fire. I followed the geysers of white steam right up to the high iron and glass roof, where they gradually lost their form and way. God's many mansions could be built up there! Then the interwoven girders of the station seemed to me like a canopy of trees. I imagined living upside down and falling through them to the open sky.

'Linka!' Dad's voice.

I ran back to where a driver was stowing our bags in his cab, and we settled in.

'Is the Queen's car like this?'

'Smaller,' replied Dad.

'Can I sit on one of those pull-down seats?'

'If you like.'

We were to meet Frieda at the Zoo in Regent's Park. She arrived late. I saw her coming, in trousers and a cotton jacket, her greying hair wrapped around her head in an untidy bun. She was thinner than last time.

'Charlie! Linka!' She hugged us in turn. It was nice. My dad paid for all of us, despite her protests, and we went through the turnstile. I went from one animal to the next. I talked to the chimps and tigers and zebras. I had a good look at the eyes of a hawk, and wondered how the grasp of his claws felt. In the reptile house I asked my dad what it was like to be bitten by a snake and the man standing next to us answered. He said he was bitten by a snake in the Malayan jungle during the war. My eyes went as sharp as the hawk's, while my dad stood gently nodding, as if his head were suddenly on a spring.

'Golly, what did it *feel* like?' I asked. The man was still alive, so it couldn't have been that bad.

'It was like being shot. You be careful, sonny, if ever you go in the jungle you lift your legs up very high, like this.'

'I'm a girl, not a boy! I do girl's kisses. See? Like this.' I stuck my lips out and wiggled them. 'Anyway that's how Hitler walks. You shouldn't walk like that even to avoid snakes. It's wicked.'

'Well I never!' said the man. 'Children these days.'

Dad said he was sorry if any offence had been caused. Frieda was laughing. I liked Frieda.

'How are you, Charlie?'

I sucked on a banana milkshake, while they chatted and took sips of tea.

'We're well, Frieda. Brightsea's just the job. Quiet for its size, but growing. It's such a relief to be out of the Big Smoke and have a house of our own.'

And then it all came out in a torrent.

'Oh Charlie, I'm sorry. That must hurt.'

'I'm past being hurt. I just don't know what to do. I was in
with a chance for the Labour Party nomination, but now they
tell me I can never get it with my wife running around like that.
Brightsea's a small place and everyone knows everyone else's
business if they have a mind to.'

'Linka, go and ask the man at the entrance for a leaflet on
the World Wildlife Fund. I'm sure I saw some.'

'I have agonized. Believe me I have, but I can't see a future
with Emma. Linka made me realize what I was waiting for. She
asked me whether Emma would get better. But I didn't want to
hope. I wanted to know: is she sick or isn't she? I assumed that
if I had the facts it would be easy to make up my mind. But today
I think there won't be any facts, and to keep hoping for them is
cowardice. I should make my decision and risk being wrong.
She's found someone else. That's not sickness! The fact is she
doesn't love me. Now's the moment for me to take my chance.

'The other day I asked myself when was I last happy, and I
realized it was back in '46, when I was stationed in Berlin. I was
twenty, and I hadn't finished my education when I was called up.
I wouldn't have gone to university, we didn't have the money, but
I would have stayed on longer. To think I was only a couple of
years older than Linka when I left school. So there I was, an
ignorant fool, helping to re-educate the Germans! I learned more
in those two years when I was driving the Head Man about Berlin
than in my whole life. I saw my first Shakespeare play. I heard
Furtwängler and von Karajan conduct. They did the chorus of
the slaves from *Aida* and the release of the prisoners from *Fidelio*

almost every week, because, as the Head Man said, music really can persuade people of the attraction of freedom.

'Major-General Richards, sir! I was on his staff. I could drive, I could fix things, I learned to speak some German. Above all I liked what we had to do in Berlin and I felt for the Germans. That counted with him. We called him the Head Man because in civilian life he was headmaster of a public school. Now he was headmaster to all of us. His job was to tell us what to do to rebuild a broken country. He said, "The Germans must do it. We're just here to help them."

'He encouraged us, and it worked a treat with lads like me. And he didn't have too many rules. I mean, we all fraternized with the other side. It was strictly against regulations but it made for a good atmosphere. Richards never had a frat. I would have known, as his driver. But the rest of us had frats. It was only natural. I've never known a freer and more interesting life than we led in Berlin.

'There was lots of fuss in the papers back home that we lived too well. Everyone knew the Germans were starving. You only had to walk down the road in Berlin and you would see the pinched, white faces poking out of overcrowded basements, and the Russian zone was worse still. Some journalists made it seem as if we had swept in as the ruling class to subjugate the new poor. But the Head Man said they could write what they liked, he knew we were getting things done. Apart from that, how each man lived in Berlin was his business, with respect to the privileges he was offered.

'Before I met the Head Man I was in the Labour Party because I thought the working man had a poor deal. Our lives when we were kids were hard. I don't know how my mother managed. Now I'm a socialist for a bigger reason. Politics is about what you think of your fellow human beings and what you want for them, and that comes down to your view of yourself and the chances you've missed or taken. It's not just another way to get rich, to be noticed, to be a public someone. That's not for me.

'I did love Emma, I'm sure I did. But I would have married Grete first had I not been posted home and demobbed. I met Emma too soon after that. She was so exotic and beautiful I thought of her as my real chance. There weren't many women like her in the whole world and I panicked when I got back to England because I felt my options closing. Over there we had responsibilities and experiences which took us far beyond our years. I was twenty! But back in England I was a nobody, with no role. I had to get a clerical job just to survive. I didn't know I couldn't make Emma happy. I hoped her gaiety would carry us both along. Then I thought it would help if we had a child.

'Mavis has been helping me decide what to do. Brightsea is going in for one of these twin-town schemes. The place over there is Heilsheim, on the Rhine. They need someone to go and liaise with the locals for a few weeks this summer. Prepare the ground, make the right contacts, create an atmosphere of goodwill. I could do it if I dropped my bid to be the parliamentary candidate, and since I have to anyway, it would be better to change course now.'

'You feel love for the underdog, Charlie. You're a real Englishman.'

'The Germans are hardly underdogs any more. They've made huge, huge progress since the end of the war. I don't expect I'll recognize the place. But Frieda, you know what I'm going to ask. You like Linka. You said just now you wanted to get away. Won't you come to Brightsea for the summer and keep an eye on her?'

'Are you going to leave Emma?'

'I don't know...' He looked around the empty café. 'You're right, Frieda, that I loved Germany in its suffering years. I think I loved what it gave me. It was my first taste of a wider world and the first time I really saw the choices open to me. And when I think about it now, everything I value comes from that time – education, equality, a dignified life for all, good leadership, a sense of the wide world, knowledge of foreign countries and languages. It's what I want for Linka too, when she grows up.

'On only my second day in Germany I was travelling on the train from the British Headquarters on the Rhine to Charlottenburg. In the early morning the train stopped at a village. The order was given for us soldiers to pick up our rations. The obscure stop was to avoid the swarms of beggars who crowded round the big stations. When we stopped at that *dorf* somewhere in the back of beyond, kids still appeared, only not so many. They made a funny din: *"Hast du was für uns, Tommy? Vat you got? We have Hunger, Tommy."* The men threw slices of apple or some squares of chocolate out of the window and watched the kids scramble to find them. A right scrum it was, and they watched the kids behave like zoo animals at feeding time. Just like here. But there was another chap who spoke German and he did it differently. He got off the train to talk to the children. They were dead scared at first and ran away. So he shouted, in German, *"Hier bleiben!"* Stay here!

'The whole platform fell silent. *"Du sprichst Deutsch, Tommy,"* one cried. You speak German.

'His name was Bobby. I never saw him again after that journey, but I never forgot how he explained to those German kids that, *jawohl*, he had things for them, but they were going to have to share. He got the boldest child to break a chocolate bar into three and hand the pieces out. Equal pieces, mind! Those children will be young adults today. I bet they remember Bobby. He saved their dignity. I have difficulty explaining my socialism these days, except when I remember that story. I date my real politics from that moment. Before that I had just a few borrowed notions about Them and Us, and about the scandal of many people going hungry. It was only natural for my generation. My father was out of work. Later he disappeared and my mother had to feed four of us.

'I saw something in Berlin, when in the freezing winter of '47, sixty thousand people died. We might not have cared. They were Germans who had tried to destroy our world, Germans who had bombed our cities. But in the end the difference between winners and losers didn't matter much. The people who know most about dignity are those who are for ever tied together as victor and vanquished. That's what brotherhood means. Not that rot Peter Cannis spouts. The victor can give the vanquished man back his self-respect. The vanquished man can make the victor discover his humanity.

'In Berlin in those days, dignity turned on two things we all encountered daily: hunger and the *Fragebogen*. The *Fragebogen* – the questionnaire – was a German word all of us Brits knew. It was the piece of paper that demanded, Who are you? Who are you really? And then there were the interviews we conducted to ask the question over and over. Germans who wanted anything from the authorities had to fill one out, detailing their past. To get a permit to publish, to start up a business, to go back on stage, to move from one city to another, a German had to fill in an application form and then be interviewed by us. The Head Man let me sit in on some interviews. Most of the applicants would slice off a piece of themselves in the blink of an eye. They would talk about "the Germans" as if they themselves were Africans or Finns. "Only Germans behave like that, Herr Oberleutnant. I would never do so."

'I've been trying to apply the lesson to myself. Who are you, Charles Beecham? Are you a good man with a sense of your own dignity? Or are you a callous brute who deserts the sick?'

'You met Ceri, Charlie?'

'Of course. She was at our wedding. We would have got on! I like energetic, determined women. But after her first stroke there wasn't much of her left.'

'Mother had so much energy when she was younger. She could have achieved all she wanted if she'd been born in a different age. She realized it only when the war came. Emma was a late child. Mother was forty when Emma was born. Mother had a good war. Her youngest daughter didn't. The separation broke something in Emma but it wasn't Ceri's fault. Evacuation was like that.'

'Do you want to tell me that Emma is ill?'

'I want to tell you she's made a certain way. She was a restless child and could never concentrate at school. She told lies, that she had a part in a film, that she was going to marry an Arab prince, that we were all going to move to America. People said it was to do with losing Dorothy. But I don't know. She could disengage from reality. She could switch off from being responsible for herself. I'm a bit like that and

Dorothy was wholly like that. But what does that make me and Emma?'

'You make me laugh, Frieda. You're the most admirable woman...'

'But what do you think of my pictures, Charlie? What do you see there? You don't like them, do you?'

Charles had told Mavis that he hated Frieda's pictures. He found them ugly and depressing. He especially didn't like the queue of shuffling figures whom Emma said were going to the gas chamber.

'No, I don't like them because I need a certain optimism to live. In Germany I was part of the rebuilding programme and it suited my character. Others came at the time and saw something different. You're an artist, Frieda. You think it's trivial to be optimistic. But I always felt for people who were worse off than me and after I had my Berlin education I felt I could do something to help. When Emma realized what I was like she took to saying, "You're so boring, Charlie. I hate do-gooders. We're in this life to give ourselves a good time."

"The two don't rule each other out," I would reply but the way my words came out made me hate myself.

'Oh, that Berlin! It was like a play setting and yet it made me feel so alive. The city when I arrived, in winter, when it was cold with an icy blue sky, was hushed to a whisper. You heard a door slam from streets away, or a baby cry, or a tram clang its bell, and the tap tap of the *Trummerfrauen* knocking mortar off piles of collapsed bricks. We became sun-worshippers, because on grey days everything was too desolate. Life on a grey day made us onlookers in a condemned man's cell. On a bright day it seemed more like an overcrowded repair shop where we had been sent to take down details of work not yet completed. We went back to our women in the evening, women with whom we could only have a halting conversation. We believed we would get things right in the end.

'The Head Man ran a team whose job it was to try to judge people's characters. His Nazi detectors learned to read faces. They would always ask to see an old photograph of the applicant, from times when he or she was not half-starved. They would try to assess what this person was like in fit times: aggressive, cruel, kind? It was an imperfect science, but it made all of us around the Head Man interested in people, and in ourselves. I stared at my face in the mirror and for the first time tried to be honest about what I saw there: not a strong character, but an honest one. I had the guts to say no, though I doubt I would have resisted the Nazis myself, not openly anyway. I'm not so much of an individual.

'I thought about myself as I trekked to the Mess building, which was on the Kaiserdammstrasse. It was a former Nazi SS drill hall and no one had bothered to remove the eagle with a swastika in its claws over the entrance. The waitresses served us porridge and eggs and bacon. They brought us marmalade and salted butter and English toast, and tea with milk. I saved as much of it as was portable for Grete. Grete was my love. My frat!

'The Head Man called me "my boy" but I got used to that. He had been taught to like himself, not to lack confidence and I came to respect him and to regret things about myself. Public school, of course. But he wanted democracy and education, and he had this way of speaking to you, which made you feel cleverer than you were. You know, Frieda, if someone one day writes the history of that time they will have to describe that strange brief cultural flowering, in the ruins of the German and British Empires, that happened in the British sector in Berlin, like leaves sprouting on a not quite dead tree. We had a Shakespeare Circle. We read *Hamlet*, and I can still hear '"To be or not to be" delivered in a German accent. We had libraries for our use, run by German staff. The Head Man said that in trying to get things right that was the best we could do, to make the best of ourselves. He read Milton every night.

'But now I'm back where I was always meant to be, in an office, doing nothing important. I'm the same as the others outside, but inside no one's like me. I wanted to enter British politics. I thought I could give it exactly what I had, that is, an ordinary background but some special feeling for Europe. I know now. I'm like Gaitskell, oh, not on his level of course, but there's something we have in common. The fact is that in the grass roots Party there's barely a place for us. And then all this happened. I wonder what would happen to *him* if his wife had an affair!

'Look, I have to take a chance. I have to get away. It's only a few weeks. I know, by going away I'm suggesting she's not ill at all, that she can cope. But that's what I mean by my dilemma. I simply don't know and not knowing is paralysing me. There's huge evidence for her craziness and yet no one, not even me, is quite convinced. Oh Frailty, thy name is woman! Emma lives in a fantastic version of the past and holds it out to herself as the viable future. She's full of a strange energy going nowhere, just round and round inside her. The energy makes her happy. She dances. She laughs. Yes, it's "a madness with method in it! She's like Hamlet and his mother rolled into one. I looked up the lines. She's like Hamlet because she sometimes experiences "a happiness that often madness hits on, which reason and sanity could not so prosperously be deliver'd of". Like Gertrude she is guilty! But Linka and I have no part to play. We're outcasts from her private paradise. My present life is just too painful. I can't go on.'

I slid off Frieda's lap and she stood up to smooth her skirt.

'Is this the new mini-skirt we hear so much about?' Dad asked. I reminded him to take the WWF leaflet with us if we were going to join.

Frieda laughed and offered Dad a cigarette from a silver case. 'Do you like it?'

'I do.'

'Beech, who can I meet? Don't you have friends? It's lonely work being a painter. Enough for the painter in me, but not enough for the woman.'

'Well, fancy that! One of my Party colleagues was asking about "The Electric Woman". He's about sixty, a nice fellow but a bit old for you. Actually he's a wreck. He spent a couple of years in prison for being a conshy. Drinks too much. Smokes too much. I don't say this seriously, Frieda.'

'I would like to come down sometime.'

'You would?'

'Mmm.' Frieda turned to me. I had her attention at last. We talked about suffragettes. 'Most women still feel they have a lot to fight for, Linka.'

My dad shook his head. 'I'd like to see Emma doing anything so determined as fight for her feminine rights.'

'Make no mistake, Charlie, if she wasn't as she is she'd be out there at the front of the campaign. She'd be Ceri's daughter and more. Don't underestimate us, brother-in-law! Women can too easily lead boring lives, their talents stifled and ridiculed. The suffragettes weren't crazy, they were desperate, as many women are now, who want to be more than just wives. What they were trying to bring about was a revolution, and show me a revolution without violence.'

Through Frieda's talk of art and independence and eman-cipation I marvelled at a new way of seeing myself and my mother.

'So you'd like to come down, Frieda?'

'If I came down Emma would have to agree, of course.'

'She wouldn't object. She hates the responsibility of looking after a child.'

'I could bring my paints.'

'Linka would love that. Say goodbye to Auntie Frieda.'

'Goodbye, Frieda.'

On the way back to the station the black taxis had orange indicators either side, which flicked out like a blackbird pointing its beak. London was full of low-flying blackbirds crossing each other's paths.

'Shouldn't we take care of Mum, Dad? Perhaps she should go to hospital.'

'You shouldn't believe all she says.'

'But you said she was ill.'

'Well, she is. But not like that.' We passed through Trafalgar Square, where I counted 103 pigeons before the lights changed.

Back in the train I reflected I didn't mind Dad going away. I liked Frieda. I hoped she would come. As for my mum, well, now she had Henryk she wouldn't be ill any more.

Two

Henryk couldn't wait. He was with us in minutes, and twirled her round in his arms. I watched from the ash trees.

One of the first things they did was to fold up the dining table and carry it to the hall, to make more space for dancing.

'Yaaraaaah!' Emma's guilt and fear did not last long.

From that moment to the end of the summer they seemed to remain barefoot, and all the windows of the house welcomed in the world outside.

They sometimes forgot to close the French windows even at night and I would come down in the morning into a draught of air so deep and fresh it was like diving into a cold spring. The skin on my taut face exulted. The objects in our sitting room, the turquoise modern chair, the clock and the television, were new and sharp in the earliest morning, but if I came later they were already dissolving, losing definition to the bright light. Our house began to merge with the garden, and the garden with the wild land beyond, because the doors were never closed. The field and the forest had found each other at last, as I had long wished.

'My dear Emma, some enchanted summer! You have found your stranger across the road!' Henryk sang in his light, wobbly tenor.

'The moment is yours, the moment is mine, now and for ever!' she sang back.

They danced and I went barefoot and barelegged too, never dressed in more than shorts and a T-shirt. When we sat out at night on the crazy paving patio, which my father had so carefully constructed, the stone had stored so much heat from the day that I contrived to set every possible inch of my exposed skin in contact with it. I lay down flat, with my legs splayed, as if I had a huge warm animal beneath me, and stared at the darkening sky. The sound of birds and the occasional sentence from Mrs Girton's television mingled with the wireless and chatter from the kitchen, where, under a bright electric bulb, Emma and Henryk were loading our bread and cheese and tomatoes on to a tray. Since neither knew how to cook, but really because they wanted a more natural existence, all our meals for the next weeks were picnics, without knives and forks.

'That was so much easier,' breathed my mum, with satisfaction. They drank lager, and gin and tonic with ice, and sat or stood in the garden.

'Let's go for a little walk, Emma.' He urged her in the direction of the ash trees. My fellow acrobats who functioned as a mute chorus in our house drama almost smiled.

'Mum won't be able to get across there. It's too steep. You'll have to go round.'

'Which way, Linka? Show us!'

I marched out the house and round to show them the path that ran along the side of Mrs Girton's. 'Mind the ground in the field. It's very bumpy though you can't see the bottom for all the grass. And there are rabbit holes!' I was now their joint protector, and off and on Henryk, with one of his selves, was mine in that he offered me the wisest explanations of the world I had ever heard.

'You remember that pit you once climbed into?' he said to me when we were alone in the same spot one morning. Often she liked to 'get up alone', even with him, and preferred no one to be in the house. 'Your mother is like a creature at the bottom of the pit. She has to help herself climb out but she can't. Not like you. Your mummy is like that. She wants to get out into life but she can't.'

'Because she's not modern enough?' But I knew already that was not the answer.

It was a beautiful fresh day with a slight wind blowing wafer-thin clouds across a blue sky, and since the grass was damp we squatted on our heels. Henryk after a while observed that he liked the nature. I frowned. 'It's not *the* nature. Just nature.'

Then Sen's red jumper caught my eye on the hill leading up to the Watchtower tree.

'You know him?'

'It's Sen. He just wanders about. He doesn't have a career or anything like that. And I don't think he ever went to school.'

'You like watching people, Linka.'

'To know what might happen. I'm sometimes afraid.'

He stroked my head. 'Yes, I can see.'

But Sen reminded me of something else. 'Have you still got the gun you were wearing in the photograph?'

He sighed. 'I'm a strange man. Yes, I have. A sort of souvenir.'

Then Frieda came, and we welcomed her as we had sent off Dad.

'Darling! You look lovely as always.' Hugging my mum, she put her grip down in the hall and turned fondly to me. 'Hello, Linka, you've grown. I expect you hate people saying that.'

'There are only a few things I hate,' said Mum. 'One is when my daughter is called that name.'

'Oh come on, sister, loosen up a little. You wouldn't want to be called a name you don't like.'

'It's common to shorten names.'

'That's rubbish.'

My mother's snobbery was fake rationality, Henryk said, a kind of good order of life she had invented to cover her struggling days. I smiled at Frieda who also found this edifice fallible. Especially as my mum in her happier moments was more what the next half-generation would call a hippie than a snob. In fact, both my parents had their natural inclinations and also whatever they thought was proper, but culture and nature got so muddled that their prejudices crossed over each other. My mother in her revolutionary modern mood said family relationships were no different from others, nor did one need to defer to one's elders and betters, since this was no longer Victorian England. Yet she decried sloppiness and whatever she called common. Dad, on the contrary, had respect for the established order of things, such as he had learned from the Head Man, and still he felt it his task to hate class distinctions and fight against privilege. He couldn't find a place in politics for his views, and yet he wanted to fit in. Henryk entered our tense and muddled little world with the great advantage of being a foreigner.

Frieda turned to my mother. 'Well, darling, so Charles has gone away! I'm sorry to have missed him. I always had a soft spot for Charles. Are you getting divorced? Do tell!'

Frieda was more sure of herself than my mother and focused hard on the person she was talking to. My mother tended to drift away.

'What about you? Still no replacement for James?'

Frieda shook her head mockingly. 'I'm so hopeless. Who would want me?'

She wore beige cotton trousers and a yellow shirt with heavy orange beads, and with her earrings and her loose, longish hair curling here and escaping there, she was a mass of interesting detail. Some grey hair showed. She flopped into our modern armless chair and kicked off her shoes, revealing orange-painted toenails. Mum sent me to fetch cold drinks.

Of course, my mother would not want to tell everything straight away. I don't think she really enjoyed talking.

'And how is life?'

'Not so bad. I'm having an exhibition in the autumn.'

'You never think of leaving London?'

'But it's such fun!'

'I met Charles in Trafalgar Square,' my mum mused out loud. 'New Year's Eve 1947.'

At the mention of London I thought of red buses and Chelsea pensioners, Horse Guards, hotel commissionaires or anyone in a uniform, and glittering shops, and the cartoon theatre with the Pathé News Reel at the station, and the Queen. *I promise to do my duty to God and the Queen. Churchill's time has passed. Britain must be part of Europe.*

'Have you been to the War Museum, Frieda?' I sat cross-legged, between them, on the floor.

'Oh, this child!' yelled Mum, as if I wasn't there. 'Linka, couldn't you—?'

'No, I want to listen.'

'Not your fault at all, darling. I suppose you jumped in the fountain together?'

'I can jump,' I said, and went out into the hall and hurled myself off the fifth stair up.

But Frieda misjudged my mum's mood, which, by the time I came back into the room, had suddenly become regretful and nostalgic. 'You used to be very unkind, Frieda.'

Frieda recognized 'the change factor' at once, as 'of the family', 'in the genes', though she didn't say so. Some curious, unsettling factor had lodged under her sister's skin, which meant that nothing in nature or human invention could comfort her. 'I know, darling, I used to tease you about Dorothy coming to get you in the night. I'm so sorry. It used to frighten you so.'

'Well, don't do it now.'

Many shadows hung over us, and with Frieda stirring the whole issue of family, Dorothy's took on a firmer outline.

I took Frieda's grip upstairs for her.

But then I had to intercept her coming upstairs. 'Wait, Frieda...' I dashed past her out to the garage, and back upstairs again trying to conceal the hammer behind my back. 'People in a Waiting Room' now hung slightly askew on the long wall of the spare room.

'Aah, you're a good girl,' she said. 'No one likes that picture. It reminds them of Hell. But I think it's just the life they can't face.'

'Like not being able to face being dead?' I thought of the woodpecker; just bones and night.

'It's not quite as bad as that!' laughed Frieda.

I sat for a moment, while she unpacked. The incident in O'Brien's shed, and stealing wood for my tree den reminded me I wasn't wholly a good girl. But with part of me I was, and never more so than now, in our house, because Dad was absent and someone had to replace him.

'Is this picture your own younaded effort?' I asked at length, still staring at the bent and twisted figures in the queue for nothingness. 'You know, when you don't have anyone to help you.'

'Unaided', I meant. The word formed part of the written conditions for entering competitions based on knowledge, not fate, in children's newspapers and comics.

Frieda straightened my hunched shoulders. 'You're like I was as a child, Linka, about the same shape and size. Perhaps you'll grow up to be a painter.'

I took a deep breath. 'I hope you don't mind my saying, Frieda, but I like the picture downstairs better. And actually I'm going to be an architect and design houses which perfectly fit in with nature.'

She smoothed my hair. 'You have the chance, darling. I hope you do. And keep going in for those competitions.'

'Mummy doesn't like "People in a Waiting Room" because she says it's where she is. That it's her fate.'

'She shouldn't talk to you like that. They're grown-up things.'

'But you do sometimes, and I like it. It's interesting.'

I wouldn't let go, and in the end I got Frieda to agree.

She brought out a bottle of sherry from her grip and took it

downstairs. We got out some glasses and I was allowed to sip.
She smoked her cigarette through an elegant holder. When my
mother got into a better mood, as now, she and Frieda made an
attractive pair, and they talked their way through the whole of
Vogue, commenting together on each page.

'Oh, chic, darling, chic!'

'Of course, there are those who go on about the Bomb, and
think another war is just around the corner, and who knows,
they may be right, in which case make hay while the sun shines,
I say. Do, Emma. You'd be sorry to get to forty like me and have
passed up the chance.'

'You had James.'

'And I paid for it. Don't ever trust a married man.'

'Didn't he love you?'

'He lacked courage.'

Poor Frieda, I thought. She's lost something. Also, everyone
should be brave. Down with all cowards!

Mum said, 'I don't know about love. It's pleasure that
counts. Real pleasure. I'd forgotten it existed. No, I never knew
it could be like that. The joy, the ecstasy of waiting, the
trembling of beginning and a long, long happening, then
floating away and peace.'

Frieda found that too much in my presence, and raised a
finger to her lips.

We heard a man's voice. 'Halloh?' These days Henryk just
walked in through the back door, or came in through the French
windows with a tap and a hallo, which sounded foreign because
he never cared to give it an English 'o'. 'Halloh?'

Frieda got up barefoot from where she had been reading and
shook his hand. I found myself thinking again that she was

attractive, but in a different way from my mum, and in a way more successfully, because it was as if she had found a language into which to translate Mum's dancing, and through this personality she could make contact with people. Also she was not attacked by those sudden anxieties Mum was prey to, which reversed all the expected priorities and left her locked in herself or at the bottom of the pit.

'We're having a nice time, Henryk. May I call you Henryk? Why don't you come and join us?'

'I have to work tonight, Freedar.'

'Surely you don't have to work all summer. We need a man to entertain us.'

He laughed. 'Someone's got to go to work.'

'No, he doesn't! Who needs money when you've got sunshine?'

I thought of the crinkly brown ten-shilling note Frieda had given me and Dad's saying people made too much fuss about money.

Mum pulled Henryk down beside her by his tie and kissed him and murmured something about going quickly upstairs. He agreed. I thought Frieda was shocked, so I got out the Monopoly. It's not so good when you have only two players, but it passes the time.

'Our mother looked like Linka, don't you think, Emma?' Frieda said later. Again, my mother never terribly liked talking about her childhood, but with Frieda there, whom she had invited, the subject was inevitable and self-inflicted.

'Our mother neglected you. But then you came so late. She thought she'd finished having a family then.' Frieda stopped and started again, and then somehow saw clearly the thought that had been slowly taking shape as she switched backward and forward in her mind. 'Emma, I've always thought you needed a hobby, or a job.'

My mother was exasperated. 'Frieda, don't keep telling me what to do! You sound like Charles.'

'But Mummy left you feeling so uncertain. The problem was she was too dominant and determined, Emma. They would have loved Ceri in the Navy! She was a real pioneer, feminist, you name it, and beautiful too, and terribly mean to Daddy. Look at poor Daddy, poor downtrodden sod! We couldn't copy Ceri in seeking out our men, so you tried staying a little girl, and I became a painter! And now you're like this!'

'That's enough, Frieda, in front of Lynne-Caroline. I think you're quite drunk.'

'That's rich, coming from you! Is there any subject on earth you don't discuss in front of your daughter? If I were her mother...'

Emma hid first behind me and then her own cloak of snobbery. Frieda had her own problems. She wasn't drunk, but she drank more than Emma and persisted for a while. "Sooner murder an infant in its cradle than nurse unacted desires." Did you ever read Blake at school? Not that yours are unacted, darling. Henryk's gorgeous, Emma, what a hunk.'

'Goodnight, Frieda. I can't talk all night.'

'Perhaps we should go to bed, darling.'

'Yes, goodnight.'

My mum's mood switched even as they were going upstairs. 'Charles is so boring with his politics, that's the trouble. Goodness is such a bore.'

But what they were really doing when they talked was all the time seeing where bits of the family jigsaw fitted together; who was like whom, and why. The family is fate, at least my mother saw it that way. And when I saw her mentally side by side with her sister, fragments of insight came to me. It was as if the talent in her, whatever would have made her a consistent personal force, had been blasted apart and the atoms scattered, in a great diffusion of power that left each splinter of her humanity disconnected and powerless.

The next day we went to the beach. Frieda backed the Anglia out of the garage without mishap. 'Well done, Frieda, bravo!' I was impressed, because Dad had brainwashed me into thinking all women drivers were hopeless, except the one I would one day become.

'Thank you, darling, but it's not at all difficult. Emma, why don't you learn to drive?'

I feared that question and its possible answer would disrupt the whole morning, but mercifully she let it pass.

The twenty minutes it took to drive to the coast passed in lovely relaxing sunshine. The wind streamed so hard into my back window that my eyes watered. The road ran along the shore and the sea glistened beside us, like, in yet another new guise, the monster I imagined had tolerated having Esper Road built on his back and at least lent the woodpecker some bright colours for the duration of his life. My mother was in love, the field met the forest, and I loved the monster again more than I loved God. The monster taught me patience but also joy, and in that substance of his I would now swim.

We followed a well-trodden path down the grassy cliff and

set up our camp by a rock in the sand. Emma and Frieda put on
bikinis. My mother's figure was slack but not unlovely when
she was young, because she had a nice long belly, and was
always slender. A blinding light, the highest sun, emanated
from the clear sky, and reflected off the sea. If I think of myself
now, in that moment, I so much wanted her to be in love, to
have found her man, as nature intended, even if that man was
not my father. But I could never, never be sure.

Frieda said summer bleached nature, which is why she found
autumn with its crisp colours so life-restoring, but my mother
somehow took this as a criticism of the perfection of the
present moment, as if deep down she herself were harbouring
fears of a return to the more usual English clouds and rain, and
violently objected.

'Don't say that, it's ridiculous! How can you say that in the
middle of summer, when we've come out specially to enjoy this
hot day?'

I stepped in to soothe my mum's mood, just as my father
would have done.

'When you were a Wren, Frieda, did you serve on a ship? Did
you wear a uniform? Mummy was very glad she wasn't old
enough to serve in the war.'

Since it had become painful to keep looking directly at my
mother and my aunt, I scanned the horizon for a tall ship on
which to fix my fancy.

'I never left dry land, Linka, I'm ashamed to say. I spent the
whole war plotting points on maps.'

I condoled with her and we sat in peace.

We strolled to the shoreline. I put on a snorkelling mask,
floated face down, and kicked hard. When I came up from

exploring the seabed, where I had encountered two mussels and a razor shell, Frieda said, 'You never know, you might find the lost city of Atlantis down there.' I demanded an explanation and thrilled to hear it. But Mum soon got bored.

'Leave her here, Frieda. Let's go up. She can swim and she knows where we are.'

'Better not,' said Frieda, who I decided must have been a good Wren, and would be a great person to go to the cinema with. So I earned an extra five minutes of their company and vigilance before we all went back up the shore together. Then Frieda looked for patterns in the stones with me, and we collected as many different colours as we could find.

I became engrossed in the stones. The game was to find a flat one to use as an anvil, and a long, thin but strong one for a hammer, and then to pulverize different colours.

'You could make a picture, Linka, if you saved the dust. We could mix it with glue at home.'

'We'd need envelopes or bags, wouldn't we?'

'Use this.' She passed me the copy of *Vogue*. 'Tear out the pages and make pockets. You know how? Then you can label them.' I found myself tearing out pictures of beautiful, bare women and filling them up with dust.

'We'll have half an hour's peace now, Lynne-Caroline,' ordered Mum, who routinely found my curiosity about life intrusive. Her next sentence would have been about the need to send me away to school. So I went quiet.

The two sisters lay provocatively in the sun, while I tapped away behind them with an absorption that bordered on compulsion.

Frieda stretched and ran a hand down her baking thigh.

'You know what? I need a man.'

'You could share Henryk.'

Frieda leapt up. 'Henryk, darling? Why, I never thought... I don't know about you but I'm going for a swim.' I watched her running down to the sea on her strong legs.

There was a new mood in the car on the way home. It comprised a feeling of confidence all round, and sensual ease. 'Love and marriage, love and marriage, go together like a horse and carriage...' We sang, cynically on their part, and with a great deal of laughter all round, on our way back home in the Anglia. We picked up fish and chips on the way, though that made me sad, because in the past I had always gone there with Dad, and enjoyed holding the warm packages, when Mum didn't want to cook. It was a curious way to spend the summer holidays from school, and what would Miss Rogers, whom I could not imagine as ever undressing, have thought? But I lay on warm stones, and straddled warm trees, and hugged warm packages and was not unhappy. I lived in my own world, which was fine, so long as my mum was happy.

Henryk came over that evening with the news that he had taken two weeks' holiday. Frieda produced a bottle of champagne.

'Get some glasses, Lynne-Caroline. Henryk, put on some music.' Emma was in her more energetic mood.

'Champagne, Linka?'

'Have you got any pop?'

'I knew I'd forgotten something.'

They talked and joked and Frieda made toasted cheese for all of us.

But then, when it was dark, Henryk said we should try

listening to something different, and that we should turn off the lights and not talk. He had evidently planned this evening, and, as the needle bumped over the first blank and gritty tracks, my heart hammered with anxiety. Then *The Rite of Spring* began winding up towards its great explosion. Spring ended up marching like an army, with every last twittering creature enlisted. I lay on the carpet with the random scattering of coloured batons. Through the open door to the garden moths flew in and banged against the glass wall into the hall, which was still lit. Henryk stretched his legs out next to Mum on the settee while Frieda sat beside them on the floor.

'It's the jungle in the blood.'

'Spring. Everything pushing up out of the earth.'

'I find it noisy and exhausting.' Oh no, The change factor. Please, be happy. Stay happy.

'Not exciting, Emma?'

'No, put the lights on.' She looked around, reassuring herself she was in a familiar place. 'Who was that painter, Frieda, who went to the South Seas? Did he really like it, do you think, living among the natives?'

But Henryk made a mistake every time he tried to show my mother something of herself in a mirror. She did not want self-knowledge. Or perhaps it is just unobtainable for a person who refuses to strive, and doesn't care to put things into words, or for that matter, to paint them. There was a sense in which my mother was under-equipped, more than most, for the task required by happiness.

I don't remember how that night ended, nor many of those nights, only that the days and evenings were mostly fun, and they were often three together. Frieda introduced something like a familiar pattern, because she had a book by Elizabeth David and became our cook for the summer.

We sat cross-legged on the carpet, eating with our fingers. 'Mmm.' Frieda was even too appreciative. Mum, in her unreflected snobbish way thought a woman shouldn't show so much appetite.

'No, Emma, it's not vulgar, it's just a sign of real appetite. A woman who can devise such sexy food as this must be a sexy woman.'

'If she hasn't given away all her sensuality to her food,' observed Henryk. 'Women are such strange, versatile creatures . . . '

'She's beautiful, look.' They passed round the book, which showed a young, well-bred face, though Mum said the sexiness of the meal, 'if you say so, Frieda', still wouldn't make her enjoy shopping.

On more relaxed days Frieda made chilli con carne, and served it from the saucepan, which she rested on a folded newspaper to spare the carpet. A pan of rice and some French bread warmed in the oven, and a big wedge of Edam cheese 'for pudding' comprised one of the first 'huge meals' in my memory. I suppose my adult palate was beginning to wake up, though I had to fan my tongue against the unaccustomed spices. Henryk joked that there was clearly no need for tables in anyone's life.

Indeed, except for a few chairs and the TV and the pick-up, the room was cleared for living. Perhaps that's why the sisters decided to redecorate it by splashing on emulsion paint over Dad's patterned wallpaper. They did it in pale orange, which produced a violent effect in combination with the red patterned carpet.

'Did you paint our room to look like the sunset, Frieda?'

'Darling, that's very clever. I didn't, but you're absolutely right.'

'It goes very nicely with the turquoise chair.'

The warm weather returned with a vengeance. Frieda looked from Mum to Henryk and back again. 'All right, never mind about books and words and music. Who's coming for a swim?'

'There speaks the artist.'

'She's on holiday.'

'But Frieda, it's dark.'

'The tide's out.'

'We'll walk down. There's no one watching at this time of night. And hell, even if there is...'

Henryk drove and it was a very warm night, with only the slightest breeze coming off the distant sea. Frieda made a neat pile of her own clothes and on the grey sand she stuck and lighted some candles. She leaned across Henryk's back to set one straight, and one of her breasts nuzzled against his left ear. The white of his buttocks looked comic as he walked with the two sisters to the sea. Somehow he always managed to walk in front of me.

The waves were no more than the tiniest wavelets, like butterfly kisses on your toes. The adults, out up to their waists, were already preoccupied with each other, shouting and jumping up and down, and splashing. The splashes festooned their antics in phosphorescent sparks. The night sea had its own source of light. My mother and her friend and my aunt were all electrified!

Lying immersed in black water was like lying in the embrace

of the forest. Then I swam again, out of my depth. Finally,
when I was tired, my feet sought and found the corrugations on
the sandy bottom. I felt the pull of my body as I waded out of
the water. The sea followed me and pushed me along. Little
breakers crashed behind my heels and threw out anklets of
sparks. Then running without clothes, I felt extraordinary
freedom, together with the pleasant friction of sand under my
feet, and between my toes. I stretched my arms up towards the
sky, and stood on tiptoe, so that the whole front of my body
was drawn taut. I was a dancer, waiting to be choreographed.
This was not yet my woman's body, but no longer a child's
either. The nipples were rounded, hard and opaline, as if nature
had spun around both the corona and the berry a translucent
cocoon.

Frieda and Mum were waving, with Henryk between them,
already in his underpants. Mum's eyes were liquid with
happiness.

'Can we hear that spring music again?' I remember asking,
but then I must have fallen asleep. It was three o'clock when I
woke up in bed. There was music coming now from next door,
but of the stoat-rat kind. Had I been able to discern it more
clearly, and know what it was, I would have distinguished the
voices of a man and two women crying out with pleasure.

Henryk Braunschweig, how would it be if I met you again
today, and we reminisced about life in 'Esper Rote'? Would you
be ashamed, or delighted that you left me with another puzzle
to solve? We were 'Freedar' 'Em-ma' and 'Leenka' to you, and
Emma fascinated you with her restlessness and her
contradictions. But when I think of you now, you seem to have

been quite passive. You were deeply attracted by her suffering, but you were never a healer.

One clue to you is in how you decided not to practise your profession. Heaven knows, doctors were needed in our country then. There were many Dr Pandraneths. You would only have had to improve your English, and resit your exams. But you decided to hang back and work at a level at which you might occasionally help people, but only where no one expected it. You wanted to have feelings, but to keep them at a distance, like a set of clothes you could put on and take off at will. In your ambulance man's uniform you would steal up on life unexpectedly and occasionally catch hold of the real thing again.

I see my mother's slender figure and brown skin, the blue shift dress, or the one of red and orange whirls, another inspiration for our room, and which centred on her stomach and made her fizzle like a Roman candle. You couldn't diagnose her any better than we could. But at least you took away some of the tension. She was sometimes like a great bird opening her wings inside a house which was too small for her. Yet she never learned to fly outdoors and all her achievements were luck rather than effort.

Cancel today! Cancel the future! she would seem to say, as if she wanted to live her life floating in a balloon, to untether all the strings and just drift. On days like that she felt herself and all around her as a burden. She could not bear the tension of their otherness, but nor too the tension of being at odds with herself. But at other times there we would all be, calmly eating buck rarebits and drinking lager, and she would be the first to deride anything fanciful.

She plucked Henryk like a daisy, then passed him on to
Frieda to shed a few more petals. She was right. She was ahead
of her time! She was progressive! Women should have the
houses and be provided with the money to give children
security and men should come and go as the women please. But
when will we organize the world like that?

'Share and share alike! That's what Mother used to say when
we were children.' Emma and Frieda giggled, as if this were the
ultimate naughty game and who was Henryk to mind? A
century ago, he would have been called a healthy man.

The sun shone and the ash trees formed a lush screen for our
goings on. The stone patio Dad built was our chamber theatre,
and our outdoor dining space, and with the heat it gave off at
night almost our animal companion. We had no rules. There
were always dishes in the sink and clothes downstairs. The
record-player was permanently plugged in, and with the lid up.
Even when we moved inside, Emma forgot about her old
snobbish insistence that we eat off plates and take care not to
drop crumbs. Looking back she derided Dad's insistence on
proper meals. He was such a square.

'Look,' said Frieda, 'his only problem is that he was brought
up not to show emotion. The working classes were. You should
help him.'

'Wouldn't you like to share him too?'

'Emma, you're crazy. I'm just making an observation. That
doesn't mean I want to share his bed.'

'Bed's the only thing,' said my mother. 'There isn't anything
else. We fuck and then we die.'

Poor Frieda. I think she could have felt she was in love that
summer, and certainly there was a lot of 'love' and pleasure,

only Emma would periodically pass on her doubts about the nature of existence.

I went on collecting my milk bottle tops to help against cruelty to animals, retrieving them from the bin when Frieda forgot. Otherwise I got used to keeping out of the way. I led a different life.

Three

Ishook my head at Robbie's timidity. 'Eight o'clock tonight. Don't tell a soul.'

'What if—'

'You've got to be there. Meet you by the sand patch.'

What evening was that? A Friday, early in August.

'Hi, Linka.' He greeted me with a little shiver. He was often cold. But he liked the adventures I set up, and defied his mother to see me.

'Lucky you were sick. They made me take down every plank.'

Robbie had dismantled our 'ugly shack in the trees' and his humiliation on my behalf 'was all Mrs Hill's fault'. Mrs Hill had tipped off the site foreman.

I pushed that phrase 'ugly shack in the trees' around inside my head. 'We still have to have a den.'

'Why, Linka? It's useless.' For our meeting we were squatting inside the future number fifty-two Esper Road. I brought the *Manual of Scouting* in my saddlebag. What a lovely thick volume it was, with lots of 'figs. 1 and 2', showing you how to do things, in stages, for God and the Queen.

'You'll see.'

I took no action that day, and Sunday Robbie wasn't allowed to play, so it must have been the afternoon of Monday, 6 August, 1961, when we still had no den to go to and it was raining again. Scouts, I had read, when they need shelter and find themselves in a wooded area, weave hurdles and then prop two hurdles against each other to make a kind of tent. 'Yes, yes, I want to make hurdles!' I danced about my little room as best I could. I consulted the manual, and memorized procedures until very late. Already, when I was reading that night, all the lights were out in the house, and all I could hear were animal squeaks from the fields, lit by a full moon.

'Look for straight branches!' I ordered. This time we took our materials directly from nature. Entering the ancient woods at the bottom of the field, we fanned out to left and right. The wood had to be young, oak or elm or ash, and not the fallen stuff that snapped when you trod on it. We had only one saw, Dad's, so at the cry of 'I've found one!' we all gathered. Alan shinned up and did the sawing. When the saw's teeth bit deep, the smell of sap sanctified our endeavour. The relenting branch splashed the hand of the woodcutter with sawdust.

And he shewed me a pure river of water of life, clear as crystal, proceeding out of the throne of God and of the Lamb.

In the midst of the street of it, and on either side of the river, was there the tree of life, which bare twelve manner of fruits, and yielded her fruit every month: and the leaves of the tree were for the healing of the nations.

And there shall be no more curse.

We needed six staves about five feet long and six a foot shorter. Of those, only the outer four had to be good and stout, for the job of the others, laid across each other as if to form a chequer board, was only to act as guides for warp and weft. Moses as a baby had endured in a basket of rushes, therefore we could. But for us bracken replaced rushes. Since even the coarsest grass was soft, and only about two foot long, we plucked and plucked at the bracken growing in mid-field until we had half a dozen featherlight bundles of those tindery russet-brown stems that neither scratched nor stung, nor pricked. The designated site for our settlement was a natural clearing surrounded by hawthorn, beyond the dinosaur. Robbie kept sneezing with his hands full and when he put his load down his face was covered with snot, which he wiped on his crimson jumper. He protested he was doing more fetching than we were.

'What do you think, nails or string?' Our bare knees were black and green from kneeling over our uneven work. Because the staves were so rough-hewn, they wouldn't lie flat on the ground, and were easily dislodged from the artifical arrangement we inflicted on them.

'Nails is easier,' said Alan, but Robbie favoured string, which we wouldn't have to steal, and we found some in his house, in the bottom drawer of the green and white kitchen unit. Saved from parcels, it was neatly done up in skeins. I found some more in our house, saved by Dad.

I picked one skein up and held it to my neck. 'Like a scarecrow's bow tie!'

'You're mad, Linka Beecham.' That was Danny, who 'had

come to watch'. Word had got around of my plan, even though school was over.

We bound each wood joint, and the result was a hurdle, which stood almost four square, with only a slight lunge to one side. As for the weaving, that was easy. Put together enough of the matchstick sentries that, around Esper Road at least, guard a child if she chooses to spend the night in a ditch, pack them in tight, hold them fast, and you have a real defensive wall.

'What are you going to do for the floor?' Alan liked to ask questions which pointed up my omissions and failings. He didn't have the answers, but his questions gave him a role.

'Newspaper,' I said. 'I'll fetch some next time I go home.'

My tent was completed next day. We made two more hurdles and rested them against each other to form a shelter with a triangular entrance and back wall. The enclosed tent wasn't a perfect shape; the corners of the back hurdle stuck up like two triangular ears. But of course! They were natural points on which to emblazon my colours. My paintbox and pages from my scrapbook would do so long as it didn't rain. Careless now, long beyond the pursuit of a perfect imitation of nature, I painted some kind of woodpecker in bright red and green, and stapled it to the right 'ear', while on the left, like a tail, I painted three fat green and red stripes. Then I crawled inside. I hadn't been there a minute, sitting musing cross-legged on discarded copies of *The News Chronicle* (from the Hills) and *The Brightsea Times* (from us), when I knew I should never let anyone else in with me. For company there would be Moses, ripped from the Old Testament book I never returned to Miss Rogers. I left the others to assemble their smaller tents at a distance around mine.

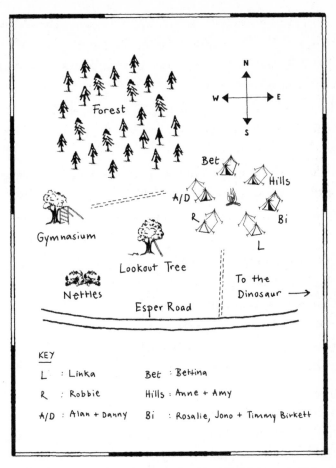

We had a first campfire. I enjoyed seeing Robbie and Al in that thrilling orange glow and basking in the summer night, even while I knew I had become two people. There was the one who wanted to understand the world. But the other person was frustrated by understanding and needed to take action.

And there shall be no more curse.

'Henryk?'
    'Yes, Linka?'

'I believe I'm everywhere when I'm in once place. I don't need to search like my mother. I don't need to be unhappy. I feel it. I'm here and there and everywhere. And it doesn't matter what time it is.'

He put a hand on my shoulder. No more curse in the eternal present of understanding.

Now we turned our attention to practical things. The fire, lit under an old metal grille we found on the fringes of the building site and supported with bricks, enabled us to warm up tins of Heinz sausages and beans. I took a couple of pans and some plates and spoons from home.

'We must have some more people. Three's not enough.'

'You always want to boss people.'

'I don't! It's not real otherwise.'

So we asked Danny back and he brought Bettina.

Bettina kept saying she was tired and giggling and going into Danny's tent with him 'for a rest'. Anne Hill was much better. In record time she made one tent big enough for both herself and Amy, and the weaving was absolutely straight and even.

'Does your mum know you're here, with us?'

'What she doesn't know she doesn't worry about. Besides, she likes us to get out in the fresh air.' Anne Hill's blue eyes lit up. She had strength and intelligence. She ought to have been my best friend.

Now there was my hut, a prominent, awkward, overlarge thing, and four others. Danny and Alan decided to share. They built Bettina one of her own. The three Birketts were still busy.

'Timmy, that's hopeless!' The boy in navy shorts and a blue and white check shirt was just waving bits of grass about and grinning, while Jono was placidly bending bracken. Rosalie got a good tight hold with her string.

'He's only five, Linka.'

'Nonsense. If Jono can do it, so can Timmy.'

'But,' Rosalie whispered in my ear, 'Timmy's backward.'

I knew that but I wasn't standing for it. Next thing they'd be saying he was mad.

'Timmy, if you don't do some work you can't be part of this camp. You'll have to go home.'

He began to cry, and Rosalie wrinkled her nose at me. Unlike older children and adults, the little ones cry from nowhere. 'Cry-baby!'

However, I already knew that if the camp was to be real we couldn't afford numerically to send Timmy home, so I took over his weaving, and soon the Birkett trio were lodged. We built a whole village in a matter of ten days. As I worked I listened to Robbie sneezing. Once our civilization had progressed and become stable, I would encourage the search for a hayfever cure, testing the natural remedies of the forest.

'She's always changing. And always wanting to be somewhere else. Sort of dreaming, but hating it when other people dream. Often finding other people hateful just because they exist.'

'She thinks she's in the wrong place. She feels great tension in herself, which comes from having to share the world with other people. So she has to love or hate them. Either way, she needs people more than you or I do. Life for her is either passionate or dead.'

'What place should she be in then?'

'I don't know, Linka. I would have to be God to know.'

'You don't believe in God.'
And there shall be no more curse.

There must be rules!

No crying!
No being lazy!
No lying!
No madness!
No stealing!
No kissing!

I wrote my commandments up on pages torn from the
scrapbook, and tied one with string over the entrance to each
hut, except my own, where it hung over my bed.

'You have to fetch some more firewood, Bettina, otherwise
there's no lunch!'
    'No lunch then. My arms hurt. I can't lift another thing.'
    That morning I fetched the wood myself, but Bettina's
capacity to become easily fatigued was how the gymnasium
began, as a place where those who weren't used to giving their
all to the great outside, the fields and the forest, could build up
their strength. There was a smaller clearing next door to the
camp and there we hung the tow rope from a high branch to
swing on and strengthen our arms. Down below we made, with
little end-crosses and poles, three horses' jumps to practise
leaping over. We also had a standing competition to try to
uproot a sapling about our own height. This resembled training
to draw Excalibur, should we come across it, or be summoned.

For easier exercise we kept Rosalie's skipping rope in the hollow of the big oak tree from which the swing dangled. Bettina was good at skipping and chanted rhymes as she jumped, but she said she'd call the police if I made her hang upside down again from the low end of the overhanging branch. She was scared of falling on her head, but I said there wasn't much in her head anyway.

> Little Red Riding Hood
> Out in the forest, out in the wood
> Tell me please, what will you do
> When the bad wolf comes to you?
> I'll tell your mother
> I'll tell your dad
> That not the wolf
> But YOU are bad!

It was about me. But at least she was getting stronger.

The day proceeded as follows. Each of us was to arrive as early as he or she could after 8 a.m., with food for the day and any tools that might be useful. The milkman got quite used to my purchasing several pints, plus some eggs and bacon and bread, from his float. I took the money from my mum's purse. She didn't care. The first greeting amongst us was a salute, but we needed a form of words. We needed our own language. So one morning when all ten of us were present I arranged a morning lesson around the cold fire.

'"*Quod bis einer amabit!*" is what you use to say hello; it also means "things are going well". "*Quod bis einer amabit!*" Repeat please.'

'It sounds jolly funny to me,' said Anne Hill. 'It doesn't
mean anything.'

'You can't have been listening! I just told you what it meant.'
I lived in a world in which any sound could serve the purpose I
gave it. The sounds came from hymns, from assembly, from
books I didn't understand.

'Linka, you sound like Miss Rogers!'

I denied it, but if it were true then let it be so. I liked hearing
my beyond-language because *I* invented it, and I merged it with
some   nice-sounding   things   from   my   stamps   like
Rzeszposzpolita Polska and *Deutschland*, and *cul de sac*, which
now officially described Esper Road on a sign where it met the
main road, and *cmentarz*, the least difficult of the words
Henryk gave me. Tsmentarsh, it was supposed to sound. My
invented words swelled our forces. Each one was a presence.
The new language made everything we did special.

'*Quod bis einer amabit!* We'll also say it at the end of
meetings, before we go back to work.' They mumbled it as we
got to our feet, though I think Anne Hill only mimed.

The first practical morning job was to check the huts for
wear and tear. I made a broom with twigs and an old pole from
the building site, and it became Rosalie's next task to sweep the
clearing. Danny and Alan were assigned to carry any rubbish
we had up the hill, and leave it for the dustmen. My ambition
was to get both the dustmen and the postman to call, but that
development would have to wait until we had an established
address. The rubbish consisted of empty Spam and corned beef
tins, and pop and milk bottles and paper wrappers.

'The popman pays money back on the bottles. Take them
and leave them in our drive.'

'Who gets the money?' asked Danny.

'It goes into the camp bank for communal needs.'

'Cement arse! You don't say!'

'Bags be banker!' said Alan. I gave him a cold, warning look, which hurt him. 'Your job is to carry the rubbish, Al. You're the strongest. It's not much.'

'You're bossy!' said Bettina. 'You always were.'

I crawled into my tent and tears ran down my face. Under the low eaves of bracken, in nest-like warmth, I curled up in a ball. When I crept out, I added to the list of camp rules:

No sitting alone in huts not doing anything!
No making fun of the rules!

It was noon in the sky, one o'clock British Summer Time to the inhabitants of Esper Road and observers of Big Ben and listeners to the BBC. I tied some string round the neck of an empty pop bottle and suspended it from a hawthorn branch. 'Ting, ting, ting, ting.' The glass was an unnatural sound out in the fields and as I sounded my gong, I, Linka Beecham of the tough breed, a girl become a god, looked up importantly, as one who took her bearings only from the conditions of the heavens.

'I just want to say to everyone: you must work hard, then we can have a real camp, and good fun, and lunch. I am aware that the sun is overhead and it is time. As you see, the fire has been lit.' I bowed my head.

'*Quod bis einer amabit. Arbeitsgemeinshaft*'. Say it, please. *Arbeit* is German for work. These beautiful words will replace "For what we are about to receive…" at all future mealtimes.

Once again, please, for practice. Now let's have lunch. What has everyone brought?'

I spread out an old sheet and waited for my people to bring food for me to bless. *Arbeitsgemeinschaft*, chosen for its length and its multiplicity of sounds, came from Dad's *Hugo's Improve your German*, priced 2/6d.

'Tomato ketchup. Is that all, Al?'

'My mum couldn't spare anything else.' He looked at me as if to say, Why aren't we friends any more like we used to be, Linka?

'My mum says pop is expensive and bad for our teeth.' Amy had started wearing glasses since I saw her last and had had her fair share of visits to dentists and opticians to break her spirit. I told her to shut up. I had a good mind to tip her water out of its Tupperware pot and over her head.

The Birketts brought eggs though and doorsteps of bread in a brown paper bag, two of them sandwiched together with a wodge of lard. Robbie contributed a jar of meatpaste. I brought some more eggs.

'It's not fair, we've brought more than anyone else and you're making us share it.'

'I'll make some soup,' I suggested. 'Then there'll be enough second course to go round. Everyone off to the gym for half an hour.'

Timmy stayed put, playing with the eggs. I looked up when he cried and saw yolk and albumen and shell all over his hands and face. He looked afraid, but managed to blurt, 'Not my fault.'

I could have stood up and towered over him, but I stayed crouching, tending the soup. 'It's all right, Timmy, you can have

one of mine. Now go and play until lunch is ready.' He ran away
as if he had been given a second life.

'*Quod bis einer amabit. Cmentarz. Arbeitsgemeinschaft.*'
We said grace. There was a general muttering round the circle,
where we sat cross-legged round the fire.

'What sort of soup?' asked Rosalie.

'Dog's Willy soup.' Danny laughed and whispered something
to Alan, but the eyes of the younger children were bright with
apprehension as I dipped old clean cans into our single big
saucepan and handed them round.

'I feel sick. I don't want any lunch,' said Amy.

'Don't be silly. Have a look first.'

'Oh, Linka, it's acorns!' Her glasses, round with pink
frames, at least helped her to see. I stared at her a bit to get her
to apologize for herself.

'You get them on the National Healthy.'

'National Health, silly,' chided her sister.

The five eggs and fried bread, all fried together with lard and
divided between ten of us, were a good excuse for even me to
leave the soup. Robbie tried to please me by drinking it all, but
cut his cheek on the tin. He sat dabbing at the blood with a
dock leaf. I couldn't help laughing, which made him cry with
rage. The weather was warm, the sky blue. 'Use any soup left
over to put the fire out!' I ordered at length. The fire hissed and
popped as unwanted acorns exploded.

'Another way to put the fire out is to piss on it.' Danny went
right ahead, surrounded by at least eight startled faces who
looked at me. I wrote a new rule: No showing of private parts!

'Heh, I've got an idea. We can fill the bean tins with earth
and stack them up and make seats for the little ones. Then they

won't have to sit on the ground and we won't have to steal so many bricks.' Robbie's suggestions were always decent and concerned with the progress of our civilization.

'All right, Mr Clever Clogs Inventor, what about a toilet? Otherwise, where do we dump it?' Danny laughed and whispered in Alan's ear. Robbie blushed.

'That's a stupid question,' I replied quickly. 'It's obvious. You go away somewhere. Everyone shall behave modestly and decently.'

But they didn't behave modestly and decently and by Wednesday almost all the undesirable work of cleaning and carrying had been loaded on to Timmy and Amy, while Danny and Alan spent their days lying in the long grass, from which I saw a curl of smoke rising. 'How you doin', cement arse?' they called. Jono Birkett, on behalf of his brother, and Amy Hill were carrying the rubbish and the bottles up the hill.

In Esper Road Diana Emsworth, strolling with Macnamara, stared for a moment: 'Ah, Lynne-Caroline, how are you?'

How are *you*? I should have asked, for she had a bump. She was expecting. But I had my limits.

'Very well, Mrs Emsworth. I've moved to a new address for the summer.'

Her eyes ranged over me. 'My, how your hair has grown! And all of you.'

'We don't have a hairdresser's in my new place. But when we get really organized there will be everything. It will be a perfect place to live.'

'Does it have a name? Can we send you milk bottle tops there?' Being pregnant made her kinder. She was pleased with life.

'It's called New Warsaw.'
'Like New York!'
'Sort of.'

At number seventeen a dress of Emma's was downstairs hanging over the back of a chair, and the record-player waited to be played. I could smell Frieda's paints. There was a comb in the kitchen which must have been Henryk's. I took some cheese from the fridge and stuffed it into my trouser pockets. As many slices of bread as I could I stuffed down the front of my brassiere, between the bosoms (for as Mrs Emsworth saw, there was already no room left elsewhere). Afterwards I crossed the street and tried Henryk's back door. It was open so I walked in, checked every room, re-examined the photograph of him in his Polish Army uniform, took some cooking oil and some paraffin from the kitchen and left again.

'Do you love my mummy?'
    'Yes, Linka, I do. Like I love you.'
    'Instead of your family?'
    'The way art is instead of life. You can't understand that, can you, but I'm not able to express it in any other way.'
    I couldn't then but I know now. He too was trying to live in an eternal present that summer.

'You didn't say *Quod bis einer amabit Arbeitsgemeinschaft*.'
    'It's stupid, Linka, they're just nonsense words. I don't want to.'
    'Well, you've got to.' It pained me above all that Anne Hill said my rules and my language were nonsense. The punishment

for refusal to use the right language was two minutes in the nettles.

'Who said? That's not written down anywhere!' cried Robbie.

Amy Hill burst into tears. Danny held Anne while the other seven of us lined up in a circle around the nettles. We took her shoes and socks off and pushed her in in her knickers and T-shirt. Each time she got up someone pushed her back again. In effect, it was either me or Danny, because Alan went and sat up the hill and sucked grass while Robbie came over all weak. Little Amy was protesting so much we had to order Bettina to take her for a walk.

I watched the second hand of my watch, the birthday present from Dad. 'That's it, two minutes, let her go.' I lowered my arm, like Miss Rogers commanding a Bible reading. 'Robbie, bring some dock leaves.' But Anne Hill grabbed her clothes, spat in my face and ran home.

I withdrew to my tent for several days after that to work on the maps and the history of the camp.

Another day I was sitting with Robbie when a sparrow landed on our lookout post.

'Go on, Linka, tell him he can't sit there. I'm sure he'll obey you.'

Brave, brave Robbie! I laughed from a place inside me a long way off and didn't punish him.

He was sitting in his eyrie above the gymnasium. I shouted, 'You didn't challenge that stranger. You have to say, "*Quod bis einer amabit?*" and make it sound really frightening.'

'But it was Patrick back from his holidays. I'm coming down now anyway. It's boring being on watch.'

'But we haven't got another guard.'

'I told you, Linka, I'm bored.'

So I kept vigil alone. I was the only one who stayed all night in the camp I had officially named New Warsaw. It was frightening, but I told myself that the rustles in the bushes were wolves and cayotes, and I was as brave as any *Wagon Train* pioneer. If you want the perfect life you have to search for the place, then build your homestead. I filled the paraffin lamp from the camping shop with the stuff I had requisitioned from Henryk's kitchen and in that headache-inducing light I sat in my tent, watching Moses watch over the shadows. When I awoke at about 6 a.m., in the first full light, I stepped out into the fresh and beautiful morning. The air was good after the fumes. Sen was in the distance, sitting in the grass.

I stretched. I washed my face in the rainwater we had collected in an old enamelled bucket from the Birketts, then I went through my exercises in the gym. I felt joy at my independence and when the others arrived, in ones and twos, ambling or careering down the hill, and saluting, I thought I saw joy in their eyes too. So I held a sort of religious service at which I expressed sorrow for all the dull *unmodern* adults who had to live indoors and lead such unhappy lives, inside the houses of Esper Road. Then I declared a reading holiday.

'Oh yes, you have to read, it's important.' My plans for the Library of New Warsaw involved stealing another plank and putting books on it.

Rosalie looked at me beseechingly. 'Timmy's backward. He can't read.'

'Even so. All the more reason to try.'

'Don't say it in front of him, Linka, please.'

'Nonsense! Timmy, do you hear me, you've got to learn to read, otherwise you'll have to leave the camp, and there won't be any more nice eggs and fried bread.' Brother and sister held hands and just looked at me.

That was the day Anne Hill came back saying nothing except very softly under her breath, once as she passed me, '*Quod bis einer amabit. Arbeitsgemeinschaft.*' She said it so beautifully I forgave her for ever that gob of saliva in my eye.

'Heh! Watch out, everyone! Someone's coming NOT *Quod bis einer amabit*,' yelled Robbie. 'General alert! Action stations!'

Alan and Danny had staffs and the little ones got out their standard-issue catapults and began a frantic searching for stones.

Bob Birkett approached with his hands in the air. It was a hot day, and he was just in light trousers and a shirt, and perspiring. He had a box camera round his neck. 'Me, kimosabe, come in peace. No gun, look!'

I stood legs astride, bow and arrow poised, with my followers lined up behind me barring the opening. A fence around the whole camp was beyond our capability and means. Equally we would never have a gate which closed, only our lookout post.

'Just look at that! Have you built it all yourselves? I'd like a picture for the paper.' He showered so much praise on us that I gave in. The story ran: some kids have built their own village in the summer holidays, led by Charlie Beecham's daughter.

Miss Rogers, having read the the story in *The Brightsea Times*, came to visit us. I was brown from the sun and fit, and my hair

had grown below my ears. In the vented linen skirt, she strode
down the field as if it were her school. I stood in white shorts
and a T-shirt across the front of my tent, with my legs astride
and my arrow drawn.

She looked at me long and hard like Mrs Emsworth, but with
more feeling. 'Well Linka I always knew you'd be famous.'

And I heard in my head: 'And he shewed me a pure river of
water of life, clear as crystal, proceeding out of the throne of
God and of the Lamb. In the midst of the street of it, and on
either side of the river, was there the tree of life.'

'We must have a school of course', I told Miss Rogers. 'We
can't just build and guard our frontiers. I'd like there to be a
school like Arlingham.'

She laughed in a way I'd never seen before, as she might have
laughed sitting at home with a friend, looking back over her
years as a teacher, drawing up a balance sheet of effort and
reward. I laid down my weapons and sat with her on a
wobbling log balanced on some earth-filled bean tins.

'Miss Rogers, why did you never get married?'

'There was a rule against it, Linka. Not all rules are the right
ones.' And she kissed me on the forehead.

The postman came a while later out of curiosity. I gave him
a new map, which included a turning off Esper Road to New
Warsaw. He put it comfortingly in his pocket. 'But they won't
let you keep your camp, you know. There's talk in the road that
it's not right.' He was diverted. 'Still you're having a good
summer, young lady, and no mistake.'

Patrick came with two big friends from his old school.
'Wow! You built all that? What d'you call it?'

'New Warsaw.'

'We're a rival state. We declare war on you.' They stood there, tall, in long trousers, strangers talking to each other and not looking at us. I always knew we would have to defend ourselves.

'General order to all New Warshavians, arm yourselves! Choose from the axe, the bolas, the bow and arrow, the catapult, the cutlass, the dagger, the gun, the harpoon, the knife, the lariat, the lasso, the machete, the machine-gun, the noose, the pistol, the revolver, the sixshooter, the spear, the staff, the stave, the sword, the tomahawk, the truncheon, the whip. Man the wireless! Look to the signalling lights!'

The knife with the translucent brown handle like an eye I wore in its sheath round my waist. We had tools too: chisel, hammer and saw. At our first war meeting that evening I waved the saw in the air and made music to dance to. Waga waga wop wop. I held the saw with two hands above my head and ordered the others to run around me hollering like Indians on the warpath.

Next morning there was no physical need to peel the branches for bows and arrows, but I did it for our souls to become intoxicated with the smell of sap. We pulled strip after strip of moist bark off the ash branches and marvelled at the perfect fresh ivory beneath. Then I hammered twenty nails through a small oblong of wood, attached it to a vertical handle, and handed it to Danny as a tomahawk. He ran a finger over the nail points and whistled. My Robin Hood staff was a juicy sapling with its head sandpapered into a smooth bulb.

The catapults we fashioned from the bifurcations of trees, among the lower branches. We snapped off the small shoots and cut a slit in the top of each fork. Into the slots I inserted some knicker elastic from the workbasket Mum never used. Alas, the knots looked unprofessional. Knotted knicker elastic did not figure in the story of David and Goliath. Nor did these weapons sit comfortably in our hands. Still, it was worth a try to see if they would work. One shot carried a stone thirty yards. I heard it slam dully into a tree trunk at the bottom of the valley. Good enough. Then I went for a walk in the woods to figure out my battle plan.

'Heh, Linka!'

Sen was carrying his air gun, and, by its paws, a dead rabbit. I felt terribly sorry. He hurled the corpse into the undergrowth.

'Pesky things. There, I've done your work for you, Mr Fox. Have a nice dinner on me.'

I stared at Sen's red jumper. 'Are you sure they can't see you coming? Are rabbits colour-blind?'

'I swear they are. Besides I ain't got nothin' else! Here.' He came and stood behind me, pulled me towards him and lined up the rifle for me to shoot. 'Have a go!' I could feel his breath on my neck and his arms squeezing my ribs.

'Where shall I shoot?' I pointed the long black barrel into the endless darkness of the forest. The edge of metal dug into my shoulder, but suddenly my discomfort corresponded to a great bang, which produced a flurry of tweeting in the treetops.

'Fun, ain't it?' Sen came round to the front of me and, flushed with pleasure, opened his arms.

'But it's so loud.' I evaded his arms.

> *Wędrowiec, na istnienie spojrzawszy z ukosa*
> *Wszedł na cmentarz: śmierć, trawa, niepamięć i rosa.*

We worked some of the Polish sounds up into a frightening chant.

When drove jetz! When drove jetz! Sporshavshee
sporshavshee sporshavsheeeeeeeee! Travatravatrava. Smert
Smert Smert. Travatravatrava. Smert. Smert. Smert.

A new language was emerging on the other side of meaning.

Robbie hurried down from the lookout tree. 'We'll never
hold out!'

'Bettina!' I waved towards the hammock. 'Ring that gong.'
Her dull eyes looked around. 'The bottle, stupid, ring it.
Everyone knows the signal.'

Our merry band gathered round the ashes from the previous
night's fire. Bettina's job was to paint our faces with lipstick. I
handed out weapons.

'Linka, we can't use those. It will hurt.'

'Our mother doesn't allow us to fight.'

'You're a coward, Anne Hill, and Amy, you're no better!'

'I'm not a coward.' Anne reluctantly selected a truncheon.
'But we're Quakers.'

I thrust a stave into Bettina's hands and another into Robbie's,
which left a truncheon for me. The Birketts just stood there.

'Defend the camp and I'll fix your hut for you. It needs a
whole new hurdle.'

But they stood in a row, shaking their heads.

'Will you fight for this?' I had two florins and a sixpence,
from the money back on the pop bottles.

'No,' said Jono resolutely. 'We don't want money.'

I stamped my foot and shouted, 'In that case we'll lose the
camp. Do you want to lose the camp?'

Rosalie said, 'I don't know. Maybe if it's just a pretend
battle.'

'Pretend it's pretend! But do it now!'

'They'll beat us,' sighed Rosalie.

'No. We'll win if you're not afraid to use your weapons. Spread out now like I told you.'

Amy Hill was crying. 'Linka, I can't make this work!'

True, our catapults never were much good. I handed her a saucepan instead, while to Timmy I finally gave just the Moses picture from my tent, tied to a stick.

There were four of the enemy, with a black and red flag.

Our strategy, since we were situated at the bottom of a steep hill, and had no closed boundaries, had to be daring if we were to stand a chance. I spread my strong men – Anne, Robbie, Alan, Danny and myself – on either flank of our entrance, but quite wide of it, and some distance into the field. The weaker force stood as bait, forming a line where a gate might have been. On reflection I ordered the general abandonment of catapults and bows and arrows. It was hand-inflicted blows that counted.

The boys from the Rival State advanced like beasts of prey through the long grass.

'Don't come any closer or we'll shoot!' shouted Jono bravely. The responding salvo from the other side was laughter. Lurking in the long grass I realized we had forgotten to change the words to match our weapons. But otherwise the battle was proceeding according to plan.

'Yaaaaaaaahooooo.' Patrick uttered the command and they came at us running, pelting our decoys with stones. Timmy, hit almost immediately, dropped his standard and ran and hid. But stones run out. From the side I stole up on an alien boy who was bending to look for more and cracked him across the back with my sapling. As he turned towards me I saw it was Michael.

Cruel life! I got in another blow to his stomach, which doubled him up.

'That'll teach you. Take that!'

I hollered. That was the signal for Anne and Robbie to rise up and descend. Bettina was following her own battle plan. Good. All right. No time to quarrel. We took a target each. 'Oooh!' 'Aaargh!' I flailed about with my sapling. Oh, surely we were winning! We were going to win, coming up on those long-trousered beasts from behind. 'Yes, yes! Come on, we're winning!' I, Linka, guarding my camp, am fantastically strong. You can't beat me. You can't take away what I've built. I struck out, seeing only the enemy, not their faces.

Patrick went down on the very threshhold of New Warsaw, beneath the lookout post. I winded him with my truncheon. He had grown fat over the summer and couldn't run so well. I looked up. Michael had evaded Alan and was running towards New Warsaw from the west. But we had dug a moat and covered it over with thin sticks and grass and he fell like a tiger into a trap. We had them. I ran over and kicked Michael in the ribs. I came back to the camp and skewered Patrick to the floor. The aliens fled. Danny had inflicted on one a torrential bleeding nose. The younger children came over and joined in our victory chant, jumping up and down round the prisoners, and getting ever louder.

'*Quod bis einer amabit Arbeitsgemeinschaft Deutschland Reszposzpolita Polska Hurrah!*'

'Give in?' I cried, tingling from head to foot.

'No.'

'Kick them.'

'Yeah. I give in.'

'Both say it.'

'Yeah. We give in.'

'Louder.'

'Yeah.' Patrick was crying. 'Me too.'

'Guard them!' I ordered, and retired.

Alan's knee was bleeding, and he had a scratch across his cheek. I was still breathing heavily, lying beside him in the grass. We lay there for quite some time. I enjoyed watching his chest rise and fall.

'You're a brave leader, Linka,' Alan said eventually, and we just lay there and rested, having annointed ourselves with pink antiseptic cream. Robbie lay beside us.

I gave the order to collect wood and bracken. 'Now, let's light a fire to celebrate.' Soon the fire was crackling and the yellow flames leapt high. We risked setting the entire forest ablaze that hot August afternoon. For our victory feast we had two tins of beans and a packet of cream crackers.

I began a speech to both conquerors and conquered, but found myself taking off my shirt at the same time. The brassiere contradicted my argument, so I took that off too, and threw it into my hut. 'There's no difference between boys and girls, as we can all see.' Amy and Anne looked at each other. Robbie stared into the fire. 'But for a while, girls like us, Anne, Amy, Rosalie, Bettina and I, are going to have to be cleverer and stronger, to prove it. Meanwhile I want those who tried to destroy our new civilization to remember what happened this afternoon, and that we have ways of marking out people who declare themselves our enemies.' I wound the shirt around my left hand, for I was left-handed, and in my padded hand I took a hot fork.

'No, Linka, no!' whispered Anne Hill.

But I walked over to the prisoners, whose hands were tied above their heads to the tree trunks. Patrick on my left got wind of my plan and began to wriggle violently and snort. 'Still!' I had seen cowboys brand cattle and Miss Rogers brand these very boys for lesser crimes. I dashed back to the fire, changed my fork for a second, hotter one, and kissed the three blackened tines against Patrick's hand, then Michael's.

All ten of us planned to sleep out that night.

Trouble came about nine o'clock. Mrs Hill heard from Patrick's mother and went to alert Mrs Birkett. She met Mr Woolacott in the street. Mrs Robertson was unhappy that Al had not come home. The four of them appeared on the brow of the hill. The Hills and the Birketts trooped off. Amy and Timmy gave me secret unrepentant smiles for their first taste of real disobedience.

'Mum!' said Alan. 'You shouldn't be out in these fields at night. It's dangerous for a woman.'

'Perhaps you'd see me home then?'

No one had come to collect Danny and Bettina because they had the alibi of being with the other one. One minute they were there, the next they were gone.

'Robbie?'

'I won't leave you, Linka. I've run away to be with you.'

'But you must go. It's going to get worse. Your mum will come and mine and they'll all start quarrelling.'

Deirdre Evans didn't show up that evening. Robbie had invented a wonderful creation, Summer Scouts, which he attended for weeks on end. But back in Esper Road Mrs Hill and Susan Birkett had been banging on the front door of number seventeen until Emma wished that, like Henryk, she and Charles didn't have a number. 'All right, we're coming.'

'About time too. Shame on you, woman.'

'Lynne-Caroline, for heaven's sake! Where are your clothes? And poor Robbie, shivering. And put that thing down. I really think you should have been born a boy. I've had people complaining about you all day.' There she was, in slacks and a pretty blue shirt with squiggles, being utterly normal. Henryk stood beside her.

Out of the corner of my eye I saw Sen. I signalled to him and begged Robbie to go home. To the two grown-ups I said, 'Don't you want to see inside my tent?'

'We do,' answered Henryk. Bending over, they passed inside under the sign of the woodpecker and up to the altar of Moses. I had them. 'Guard them, Sen.'

I moved the grille where we had done our cooking and rammed a stave into the ground.

I took the gun from Sen. 'The prisoners should shimmy out on their bellies one by one!' I loosed a shot down towards the ground to show I was serious. 'Tie their hands behind their backs! Tie the man to the lookout post and the woman to the stave.'

'Lynne-Caroline, you're mad. What do you think you're doing?'

My mother stood a captive surrounded by half a dozen straw huts in the twilight. Her lover was anchored to the lookout tree a short way off. I took the paraffin, threw what was left equally over the huts and set light to them. 'Back everyone.' We withdrew, standing in line with Henryk, watching my mother encircled by fire.

Four

I was passing on my bicycle when a high, unsteady voice hailed me from the pavement.

'*Quod bis einer amabit.*'

'Stupid, you can't say that now.'

'Don't call my Timmy stupid.'

'Timmy is stupid. Some kids are.'

Susan Birkett raged at me. 'He's had to have three stitches because of your rough ways. He's human. He's made of blood and skin and bones, like you.' I saw the rough scar on his temple. The kindred brands I left on two sets of human hands marked my violent exit from childhood.

'Sorry.'

'Young ruffian.'

It was the beginning of September. The weather was still warm and dry, and with that part of me which loved nature I had no desire to go back to school. Only the fields were branded too, and I had no companions. I straddled the dinosaur and watched the bulldozers advance from the west. In a few years they would need a second postman. I climbed the Watchtower tree and, with paper folded in my pocket and a pencil, wrote a letter to Frieda about all that I could see. Frieda had left at the end of August.

'Did you have a nice holiday with us, Frieda? Wouldn't you have preferred to go to Spain?' I asked the morning she left.

'"The rain in Spain..."' she began to sing. She was energetic and melancholy and said she must get back, she had a lot to do. She and Henryk exchanged kisses on the cheek.

Robbie's mum kept taking him shopping for uniform and equipment required by the Boys' High School. Twice I signalled to him by torch late at night, but he failed to come to the window. My infamy didn't allow me to knock. I believe that not only I but my mother and Henryk were waiting for my father to come home. He was the final, though blank, piece in the jigsaw. He fitted the space, made sense of the pattern, although we no longer knew what colours and shapes filled his life. He sent me dull, happy letters about the couple he stayed with in Heilsheim and how easy it was to make German friends.

I knew my father would be there for the beginning of the school year. With the same instincts I knew he wouldn't otherwise have told a good story about what had happened to him in that faraway town on the Rhine where all the words people spoke sounded like *Deutschland* and *Arbeitsgemein-schaft*. But History made him less than a dull man. When he did arrive he came as an extraordinary messenger, and Henryk was so keen to hear more that he forgot what divided him from my father.

'Dad! You're not a prisoner in that other Germany? Hurrah!'

'Linka. What are you doing up so late?'

Emma, Henryk and I were sitting in the garden staring at the backdrop of the ash trees, as if waiting for the next act of the play to begin, or in my case staring at the endcloth, when my father appeared around the back of the house, still carrying his bags, and said, 'Well, I'm back! Linka, won't you come and give Daddy a kiss?'

Henryk stood up, and said, almost as if he had been appointed to the position he had fulfilled over the summer, 'Charless, welcome back. I was just telling your daughter about the Berlin Wall. What a terrible thing.'

Dad was the messenger, but Henryk had filled our house with newspapers. I knew about guards with guns, and a huge concrete wall topped with barbed wire, which locked in Poland behind it.

'It's terrible, Dad. Henryk can't ever go back.'

'That's a pity,' Dad replied with a twist in his voice. Mum looked away.

Germany had been divided overnight. People were trapped on the Russian side where they didn't want to be. Couples and families were divided. The Russians, long objects of deep suspicion in Esper Road, had fulfilled everyone's second worst fears and taken a portion of Germany hostage. Only Peter Cannis would say they were entitled to do this out of fear of Western aggression.

'Charles!' said Emma weakly, finally bypassing Henryk to greet her husband. She stood there, smaller than usual because barefoot. Dad came back stronger for having been away, and my mother, intimidated by the extremes of which her nature was capable, seemed to find his solidity restful.

The dining table came back into the family arena, and with it returned the occasional family meal: a roast with vegetables and a nice pudding. The record-player sat dormant with its lid down.

The kitchen had to be cleaned. I had noticed myself, when taking clean plates out of the cupboard, that our crockery was greasy, and the cutlery smeared. For several weeks something had smelt, probably the dish cloth, and some of Frieda's hair had wrapped itself round the greening tap. Dad put on an apron and scrubbed until the filth of the summer was dissolved in the pink foam of half a dozen Brillo pads.

If this was in any way an ordeal for him, he did not show it, and surely his good reception in Brightsea encouraged him to see everything for the best. *The Brightsea Times* interviewed him about his time in Germany, and the new problems facing that country. They asked him a question about me, to which he replied that we all know how difficult it is to bring up children in today's world.

'Will I have to go on trial, Henryk? Like Eichmann?' Newspapers, newspapers! Henryk was responsible for their proliferation in number seventeen Esper Road. He spent his money on them while declaring complete lack of faith in their honesty. Hitler's aide Adolf Eichmann was on trial in Jerusalem.

'No, Linka. You didn't know what you were doing.'

'I did a bit.'

We sat on Henryk's uncomfortable chairs, a gift from the Salvation Army. His blank walls were redeemed by the early autumn light. The hawthorn in the back was covered in berries, and there were blackberries on the brambles. 'You could make jam.'

'My mother would have made jam.'

We listened to Beethoven's Violin Concerto, and I felt deeply sad. I wondered whether Eichmann had an excuse like the one Henryk offered me, that it seemed to him as if it had only happened in a story.

My new school, Brightsea Girls' Grammar, lay in the opposite direction from Arlingham and took twenty minutes to reach by bus, plus a long walk uphill. Dad asked Mavis to come with him to the pre-term meeting when the headmistress addressed parents and pupils together. I heard him say to her that this moment was like putting a message into a bottle and throwing it out to sea, not knowing whether it – your child – would ever come back to you. And perhaps he did have an imagination, only it was stifled by long years of discouragement.

I sat next to the window, at the back of the classroom, and missed the smell of fresh air. The over-powered central heating in that dowdy, institutional building and the droning voice of the grey-haired history master, who compensated in volume for a speech impediment, sent me to sleep in a novel way. I thought sleeping in the day was for old people. Meanwhile I puzzled over some words Miss Rogers had lodged in my mind, that in life I should labour and not ask for any reward.

We had to sit down far too much compared with my old life, and in the beginning I missed handling tools and materials. My hands grew softer, and for the first time I had fingernails, which my mother insisted needed shaping. Then began that building lesson, which would henceforth be interminable, of how to shape things with words. My hands stayed soft, my mind hardened. The rafters of my treehouse were the bare bones of essays. The nails were clear, sharp ideas. I learned to mix and spread the smooth plaster of good grammar. My paragraphs would take the place of perfectly symmetrical, light-flooded, brightly coloured new rooms. Beauty would be like a roof covering and would perfect my shelter. Poetry would teach me to bring together old houses and new.

The music teacher was Mr Rosenbaum. I had never thought before that one could have lessons in music. He was small, certainly older than Dad, and probably Henryk too, and always wore a rather battered dark suit with a tie he slipped off when the headmistress was not around. He had sparse hair and a thin-lipped mouth that kept breaking into a smile with the enthusiasm he brought to the subject. His nickname was Einstein. He asked which composers we had heard of. I could have said Beethoven, Mozart, or Holst. But I chose Stravinsky. His energetic reaction made me blush, and the other children laughed as if I must have done something wrong.

'Good, good. But you cannot start with Stravinsky, child. This is to jump in at the beginning, like starting with James Joyce in literature. You must go back to Chaucer, and to Shakespeare, and to Mozart and Beethoven, a more harmonious age, in which mankind believed in the goodness of man.' I fell in love with Mr Rosenbaum.

I had a lot of catching up to do with solidity and ordinariness. I began to look things up in dictionaries and encyclopaedias. I consulted maps of Spain and France and Germany and Poland. When Hamlet held up the skull of Yorick and puzzled over the senseless passing of human time, I, who hoarded bones, felt I had found a new brother.

Something I learned from our music lessons filled me with

tingling horror. Mr Rosenbaum said that music, like our culture, was built on tension. But my mother can't bear tension! I kept repeating to myself all the way down the hill home, and still on the bus. She can't bear tension and therefore cannot be part of things. She's like a light which keeps going off because the fuse wire isn't strong enough. Having a weak nervous fuse is a kind of madness, not serious enough to be considered an illness but sufficient to ensure that a person can never sustain the real pleasures life has to offer. Did my father ever understand? I don't think so.

In *The Brightsea Times* I saw a picture of a new block of flats. One Saturday morning I took the same silver bus, which for four years had carried me to Arlingham, and walked instead to Westcross Row. The materials of Alan's house had been neatly stacked, including the crinkly roof. French marigolds still grew in the back garden, and there was the slowworm pot and a large jam jar with air holes punched in the lid.

'Careful there, young lady.'

But it would be years before anyone realized the danger of that lightweight material called asbestos, which pinged when you tapped it with your nail.

It wasn't until half-term that I got back out in the fields, to which in the shortest space of time I had become a stranger. The boys were now equally confined to the company of their own sex at school. Since it was half-term, that early evening must have been just before the clocks went back for winter. I have ever since marked the solstices with private cere-monies. They open and close each year's play by providing the light.

Before the trees of the forest I recalled the mystery of
Frieda's 'Electric Woman' and our past summer. The embrace
of the warm black sea was mine again, and I could still smell
plaster and paint and tar as they made the new road, and the
biscuity, meaty smell of my skin toasted by the sun. The ground
beneath my feet was burnt in a black ring. Whenever anything
like that appeared in those days people said it was a message
from outer space, but I knew better.

'Heh there, Linka, how you doin'? You're a big girl now.
Clever like. But not too clever for Sen, eh?'

When he straddled the plank beside me I showed my distaste
for that worn red jumper. Perhaps he misunderstood me but I
think anyway he had come to claim me, after months of
waiting. Sen, who couldn't write, wanted to make babies with
me. And I had my debt to pay.

'Someone might come,' I stalled.

'No one will come,' he replied. 'It doesn't 'urt, like. You know?'

And there was that great branch growing out of him as he
stood in front of me. I stood on the tin can bench with my
hands on his shoulders and my head on one side. He held me
round the middle and jabbed at me. Then the branch
disappeared as quickly as it grew. He sat on the ground staring
at it and rocking a bit with his arms round his knees, and
laughing. 'Ho, ho, that's it, Sen, done it!'

Of all the people I had met and with whom I spent my last
summer as a child, the only truly mad one was Sen, sitting there
laughing hopelessly. Sen didn't hurt me, and afterwards I toyed
with what it might be to grow up, other than wanting to wear
lipstick and being allowed into grown-up films anyway. It might
be, as Henryk said, to take all sides at once.

Henryk put his house up for sale. No one ever expected him to stay. He had first lived with a friend from the Polish airforce in Leamington Spa, then he had moved to West London, and from there to Brightsea. *Wędrowiec*. The wanderer. He gave me an envelope with a letter I should not open until I was his age when we met: forty-five! On it he stuck a triangular stamp proclaiming the technical achievements of socialism. Approaching twelve I could hardly imagine living so long, and asked him just to tell me the meaning of those two lines of verse, for I understood meaning now:

> *Wędrowiec, na istnienie spojrzawszy z ukosa*
> *Wszedł na cmentarz: śmierć, trawa, niepamięć i rosa.*

> A wanderer, looking askance at existence,
> Entered a graveyard, death, grass, oblivion and dew.

The Berlin Wall began a new era for Europe just as Henryk and Dad and Frieda and I all parted from Brightsea. Dad, it turned out, had a new girlfriend called Helga, and had only returned to Brightsea to 'wind things up'. He would oversee the twin-town arrangement, but he would do it from the Federal Republic of West Germany. He wanted to know what the Head Man thought about the division of Germany into two and wrote to him care of the school where he had been headmaster. Peace achieved, or war prepared for? A letter came back talking about peace as a leaking ship and wishing Corporal Beecham well. Henryk compared the European situation to that of a couple who divorced but continued to live under the same roof.

'This is not necessary in England,' he said. 'In England you have space. People have houses. But in Poland, for example, this is often what we have to do, because there are not enough flats and they do not build fast enough.'

I faced the uncertainty of being left alone with my mother. But then Frieda, who dropped the Carter and took the professional name of Frieda Luck, had an exhibition and sold two of her paintings for a huge sum, far more than she had expected. Her 'Borough' training with Bomberg had brought its rewards. She offered to pay for me to go away to school, where she was sure I would soon be offered a scholarship. And so I went away to a school not unlike the one Dad's Head Man ran, but for girls. I had a magnificent education, the kind people only dream about now, and then, like Herbert Luck-Carter, I lost what I had gained and took a long time to find it again.

We left my mother inscribed in her ring of fire. Half-crazed, but full of life, she stood trapped in a circle of fire on a grassy bank between Esper Road and the dark forest. These things determined my future.